Return to the Gingerbread Inn

For Matthew and Julia –

by

Betty Stewart Behringer

Betty Stewart Behringer

Library of Congress Catalog No. 92-085327
ISBN 0-932616-44-5

To Sarah, Christine,
and Jason,
and all my other
readers who enjoyed
The Gingerbread Inn

Acknowledgments

Thanks to Clarinda Harriss Raymond, Bruce Sager,
and all the others who have once again
made a manuscript into a book,
especially Dottie Mims for her patience
and her expertise;
and finally to my husband, Fred,
proof reader par excellence.

Preface

*W*e first met Peter and Amy in *The Gingerbread Inn.*

On a picnic with their parents in Chester Woods, Peter and Amy lose their way while gathering firewood. After sliding down a slope and through a cave, they find themselves in the Great Forest, a beautiful and magical land.

They make their way to the Gingerbread Inn. Here Grandmother Hollyberry takes them in from the approaching blizzard. She gives them supper and tucks them into bed. During the night two other visitors arrive at the Inn. Peter accidentally overhears their plot to kidnap someone with the aid of a secret weapon.

Others also are listening. Homer, the pet cat, and Mistress Mousie are drawn into the plot. The following day Peter, Amy, and Grandmother Hollyberry set out together on a daring journey to right a wrong and to save Santa Claus from the gnome king who is trying his best to destroy the Spirit of Christmas.

Return to the Gingerbread Inn begins a year after their previous adventure.

RETURN TO THE GINGERBREAD INN

CHAPTER ONE
Chester Woods Revisited

CHAPTER TWO
The Mysterious Stranger

CHAPTER THREE
Plans and Promises

CHAPTER FOUR
Grandmother and Blaze

CHAPTER FIVE
A Visit to the Bank

CHAPTER SIX
An Appointment Kept

CHAPTER SEVEN
Kidnapped

CHAPTER EIGHT
The Secret Cavern

CHAPTER NINE
Escape

CHAPTER TEN
A Visit at Windchime Castle

CHAPTER ELEVEN
Elfberries

CHAPTER TWELVE
Duke Ron de Lay

CHAPTER THIRTEEN
In the Round Tower

CHAPTER FOURTEEN
An Unexpected Mishap

CHAPTER FIFTEEN
In the Valley of the Trolls

CHAPTER SIXTEEN
The Troll King

CHAPTER SEVENTEEN
The Dwarfs to the Rescue

CHAPTER EIGHTEEN
At North Pole

CHAPTER NINETEEN
Return to the Gingerbread Inn

CHAPTER TWENTY
Passing the Rock

CHAPTER TWENTY-ONE
Home Again

The figure turned its head almost imperceptibly toward them, and one dark eye glared from under a hood.

Chapter 1
Chester Woods Revisited

I T WAS A SPLENDID DAY IN EARLY AUTUMN. The maple leaves were splashed with gold and crimson. The sky was a deep cloudless blue. Although it was Friday morning, school was closed so that the teachers could attend their annual state convention. Peter was in the front yard pumping air into the tires of his bicycle when Amy came out the door.

"What are you doing?" she asked her older brother.

"What does it look like?" he answered crossly. The tires of his old bike were worn out and constantly losing pressure.

"I mean what are you going to do today?"

"I don't know. Everybody's gone somewhere. Jamie's spending the weekend with his grandparents. Andy's gone fishing with his father, and Joe and Ken are off to the mountains with their Mom and Dad."

"It's like that with me, too. Nobody's home. It takes half the fun out of a holiday when everyone goes away and you're the only one left behind."

"Still, it's better than being in school." Peter picked up the pump to carry it back to the garage.

"Do you know what I wish, Peter?"

"What?"

"I wish we could go see Grandmother Hollyberry."

"How're we going to go? Nobody even believes we were ever there! Nobody believes the Great Forest or the North Pole even exist! I don't talk about it any more. When we were there, I couldn't wait to tell the gang about it. But when I did tell them, they told me I'd been dreaming or I was delirious, or else I was crazy."

"I know. It's really funny. Daddy always says 'Seeing is believing.' But everyone doesn't always see the same things. I wish we had taken some pictures or brought back something. Then they'd have to listen to us."

"Well, we didn't have a camera," said Peter, "and what in the world could we have brought home? We lost our wings in the fog."

"Maybe we could have borrowed Homer," mused Amy.

"What? Do you think Homer would want to leave the Great Forest? He was a hero. If he had come back with us, he may have lost his understanding of language as we lost our wings. Then nobody would see anything special about him and they'd think he was just some old stray cat."

"That's true," sighed Amy. "But, Peter, wouldn't you really like to go back for a visit?"

Peter straightened up and threw his leg over his bike.

"Sure, But how?"

"How did we go before?"

"By accident, I guess. Nobody really knows how we got there."

"But they *did* invite us to come back," insisted Amy.

Peter looked directly at his younger sister. For a long moment he was silent.

"We might ride out to the park and just look around a little," suggested Peter, "just in case we do find a way to get back."

"We slid down a hill on those slippery pine needles, remember?" said Amy.

"Yes," he replied, "only the hill seemed to grow longer and steeper and ended up in a cave."

"It must have been the cave that was the entrance to the Great Forest, because when we came out the other side, there we were in all that ice and snow."

The two children looked at one another. The very thought of finding the great forest again made their hearts beat faster.

"Okay," said Peter, "we'll go; but let me borrow Dad's camera, just in case!"

"Oh, Peter, I don't think you ought to do that," said Amy with a worried little frown.

"I'll be careful not to drop it," he replied. "Just think, Amy, if we do get back and I could bring home some pictures, they'd have to believe us. We'd better take our winter jackets, too, because if it's as cold there this year as last, we'll need them."

In a few minutes the children were out the door again. Peter placed the camera carefully in the basket of the bike. Then they quietly peddled down the driveway and turned right onto the road. Chester Woods was five miles from their home. Although both children had never been specifically told not to go to the forest alone, both were well aware that their parents would disapprove of their plans. So they were very careful not to say anything to anyone as they glided down the maple-lined road past the neat lawns of Dunsdale.

After riding for a mile or so they left the town behind. On both sides of the road there was gently rolling farmland – brown fields of corn stubble and green patches of winter wheat, which would grow tall and golden the following spring. The road wound on and on until at last they came to the top of a hill and saw the trees of the state park stretching out before them. In the bright noon sun of an October day, the forest glowed in the full colors of autumn splendor.

Peter and Amy coasted down the sloping road right into the park. After following the highway for another half mile, they saw a walking trail to the left and decided to explore it. Steering their bikes down this path, they soon found themselves in a strange lonely area where they had never been before. They continued to follow the trail for a mile or so, until it ended abruptly in a clearing. The children dismounted and propped their bikes against a tree. The clearing was evidently used by campers, for there were several grills set up between large stones, and there were ashes of recent campfires.

"Probably some Scouts come here," speculated Peter.

"Or maybe tramps," added Amy with a little shiver as she peered around. The clearing was surrounded by tall conifers and dense underbrush.

"This isn't where we were last fall," decided Peter, as he stared at the towering gray granite rock which rose to a height of twenty feet in the center of the clearing.

"Maybe we should go back," said Amy.

"Let's see what's on the other side of this rock."

They began to circle the boulder until they became aware of a figure huddled close to the base of the rock – a figure so gray and still that it seemed to be chiseled from the very stone. The children paused, frozen in a mixture of fear and curiosity. The figure turned its head almost imperceptibly toward them, and one dark eye glared from under a hood at the intruders.

Peter grabbed Amy's hand as they both raced back to their bikes. They jumped on and began pedaling as fast as they could down the path that led to the highway. They didn't slow down until they were once again on the maple-lined streets of Dunsdale. They finally pulled up, hot and breathless, by the town's only supermarket.

"What *was* it?" asked Amy.

"Don't know. Maybe a tramp, but it didn't look human. But whatever it was, I don't think we should ever go to Chester Woods alone any more – ever!"

"Yes," agreed Amy, "and let's not tell Mother and Daddy we ever went there."

"Okay," agreed Peter. "No need to. We won't go again, so no harm can come of not telling them."

Amy nodded and together they pedaled off toward home.

Chapter 2
The Mysterious Stranger

OCTOBER PASSED INTO NOVEMBER, with falling leaves and temperatures dipping below freezing. The winter jet stream sank lower across the weatherman's map on the nightly TV newscast, producing a threatening forecast of a long cold snowy winter.

Peter's family responsibilities included raking leaves, shoveling snow from the front walk, and carrying out the trash cans to the curb for the twice weekly pick-up. Amy's duties were to set the dinner table and clear the table after dinner, as well as to keep her room neat and orderly.

One night after dinner Mrs. Landon called to Peter, who was at work upstairs on a science project for school, to remind him that on the following day there was a trash collection. Peter reluctantly put down the colored pencils that he was using for the chart and slid into his jacket. Lifting his leg over the banister of the rear stairway, he executed a smooth glide directly to the kitchen, punctuated by a house-jarring jump as he reached the end of his ride.

"Peter, I wish you would stop that!" said his mother. "To begin with, you could have a nasty fall. At the very least you are contributing to the cracks in the wall."

"Okay, Mom, but it's fun and it gets me here so fast – something like flying instead of walking."

"Oh, dear, here we go again! Please don't start on those wings you and Amy insist you had and then lost."

"Okay, okay!" Peter frowned as he picked up the trash container and charged through the door.

"I don't know what to do with those children!" exclaimed their mother. "They still insist that this nonsense they told us is true."

"Well," replied Mr. Landon, folding his evening paper as he sipped his second cup of coffee, "whatever they believe, or whatever they experienced has not hurt them, apparently. Their grades are higher than ever. This quarter's report cards are the best they have ever brought home. And they no longer persist in talking about it constantly. So perhaps it would be best if we just ignore any casual reference to it that they might make, and eventually the big bad hobgoblin may just go away and be lost in the past, like all our childish fears and nightmares."

"I'm sure you're right, dear. I just worry about a recurrence of that horrible time when they were missing, and not having any logical explanation from them or the police or – anyone – where they were."

"Understandably. But we may never know. So let's get on with our lives, and I'm sure time will take care of it all."

Mr. Landon kissed his wife and turned to leave the room when the kitchen door flew open and Peter burst in. Slamming the door behind himself, he slid the bolt into place. His face was white and he was trembling from head to foot as he turned toward his parents.

"What on earth –?"

"It's *him*! He's right here sitting on the sidewalk by our hedge!" gasped Peter.

"It's WHO?" asked Mr. Landon.

"KING KLUTCH!" Peter whispered in terror as he looked toward the window and then ran over to pull the shade.

"Now, Peter, who is King Klutch and how did he get here?" asked his father as his mother threw up her hands in a gesture of despair.

"*You* know! I've told you before. He is the Gnome King. And I don't know how he got here, but you'd better call the police."

Amy, hearing the commotion, came downstairs to investigate.

"Amy, Amy, King Klutch is outside!"

"King Klutch?" Amy gasped, "Are you sure?"

"Now just settle down, all of you!" cried Mr. Landon. "I'll check this out. Martha, please hand me the big flashlight while I get my coat."

"Daddy, don't go out there!" pleaded Amy.

"At least take something to hit him with," urged Peter.

"Nonsense!" Mr. Landon glared at his children as he opened the kitchen door and stepped out into the darkness. Several minutes later he returned, somewhat shaken.

"Well?" asked Mrs. Landon anxiously.

"There's nobody around now, but I found this." He held out an antique leather boot with a gold buckle. "It was caught between branches of the hedge. I suppose the owner accidentally pulled it off his foot in his rush to get away."

"Dear heaven!" wailed Mrs. Landon, "whoever these people are, they are threatening our children again!"

"He's not 'people,' Mom. He's a gnome – a bad gnome. And gnomes have ears that hear better than a dog's, and they're very, very strong."

"Now we must all calm down. We'll be sure the house is locked and bolted. Peter, tonight I'll sleep in your room. Amy, you will sleep with your mother."

"Tomorrow morning we'll take this boot to the police station and tell them what happened. It very likely belongs to some homeless man who took shelter for the night by our hedge. When he heard me coming, he ran away so fast he lost this in the bush." But as he examined the odd boot, his explanation began to lose credibility even to him.

So the house was double locked and everyone retired. Lights were left burning indoors and out, yet no one slept very soundly that night.

Chapter 3
Plans and Promises

THE NEXT MORNING EVERYONE GATHERED FOR BREAKFAST in the kitchen. Today, however, there was none of the usual morning chatter or bickering as both children sat solemnly before their oatmeal.

"I believe it would be a good idea," began Mr. Landon, "to ask your mother to come and stay with us for awhile at least, Martha. There will be times when we will have to be shopping or attending some meetings, and the children must never be left alone in the house. She can bring Blaze over here, too. Even though a bench beagle isn't a doberman, it does bark when anyone comes around."

"Oh, goody! Grandma will stay with us!" cried Amy, clapping her hands.

"And Blaze too," added Peter, who yearned for a dog of his own.

"Yes, but Grandma may not spoil you with gifts and sweets and permit you to do other things that are off limits, such as late T.V." said Mr. Landon.

"I know Mother will gladly help out," replied Mrs. Landon "especially if she thinks the children are in danger."

"All right. Now here are some rules for us to follow. I want everybody to listen attentively and obey them – to the letter of the law. You know what that means?" He looked sternly at the children.

Amy shook her head, but Peter replied:

"That means no foolin' around or cheating. We have to do just what you say."

"Precisely!" said his father. "I will drive you to school each day, and your mother will pick you up when school is out. You will stand right on the steps by the front door until she pulls up to the curb. No playing in the schoolyard or anywhere else before she comes. If any stranger approaches you, duck right back into the building and walk as fast as you can to the office.

"Do not under any circumstances leave school, even if you receive a message to meet us somewhere. We, or Grandmother, will come for you ourselves. Don't go with anybody else, even someone dressed as a police person."

"The other kids are going to know something funny is going on," objected Peter. "They're going to ask questions. What'll we tell them?"

"What is going on isn't funny," his father replied grimly. "Just tell them you can't discuss things with anyone. They'll have to react any way they care to. But don't give in to peer pressure – understand?"

"I guess," said Peter sullenly.

"That's not good enough."

"Okay, I promise."

"Amy, how about you?"

Amy nodded with a very serious, frightened expression in her pretty blue eyes.

"Martha?"

"I think your ideas are very good, John, and we will certainly all do as you suggest. I'll call Mother later in the morning and ask her to come for a visit and bring Blaze. If she agrees to come, I'll pick them up around noon. After dinner tonight we'll explain to her what has happened. The guest room is comfortable, and I'm sure she'll help us out as long as we need her."

"Very well, I'll take that boot and stop by the police station on the way to the office. They might want to talk to you children."

As Amy and Peter gathered up their school books and donned their jackets, Peter whispered softly to his sister:

"Well, at least they are paying attention to what we have been trying to tell them."

"You know, Peter, I think we should say something about that day we biked to Chester Woods and saw that tramp behind the rock."

"Are you crazy? Then we'd *really* be in some kind of trouble. NO WAY! Anyhow, that was over a month ago, and it has nothing to do with this."

"Maybe yes and maybe no. Maybe that tramp was King Klutch!"

"No way! That's ridiculous!" Peter exclaimed, with more conviction in his voice than he actually felt in his mind. "Don't make things worse by telling anyone about that day, Amy. It's bad enough already. The other kids will think we're babies or delinquents – being picked up every day by our mother – and not able to set foot in the schoolyard even for a soccer game. Good grief!" He groaned aloud as he zipped up his jacket.

When they arrived at school, Mr. Landon parked the car and went directly to the office of the principal. Dr. Smith was aware of the children's mysterious disappearance the previous year, and was quite concerned by the time their father had recounted the latest event. He promised to alert the children's teachers and to keep a watchful eye out for any strangers who might be loitering around the school or playground.

The two men shook hands and parted. Mr. Landon felt somewhat relieved as he turned his car onto Main Street and drove toward the police station.

Chief Bob Johnson and Detective Erasmus Jones, having both been involved in the search for the children the previous year, were intensely interested in the new information, especially the boot and Mr. Landon's explanation of how he came by it.

"We'll check all the nearby shelters and the hospitals and send out an APB. We'll also send any fingerprints we find to the F.B.I. We'd like to talk to the children. Could we see them tonight?" asked Chief Johnson.

Mr. Landon sighed. "They insist it was a gnome king whom they met in some great forest," he replied, plainly embarrassed.

19

"The dude was wearing a very unusual boot, with what looks like a solid gold buckle – not the usual get-up of a homeless man. Maybe the kids are on to something." said Jones.

"We'll be at your house at seven tonight and listen to what they have to tell us," added Chief Johnson.

"Very well. Thank you." Mr. Landon shook hands with the two men and departed, feeling even more concerned than when he had arrived. For these men of the law were not taking lightly his children's tales, as he had been doing. This had the effect of putting a truly sinister overtone to what he had previously regarded as childish fantasy.

Chapter 4
Grandmother and Blaze

WHEN PETER AND AMY RETURNED FROM SCHOOL with their mother, their grandmother and Blaze were at the door to greet them. In true beagle fashion, Blaze was barking and jumping all over them joyfully, panting and licking them with doggie kisses. Peter went to the hall cupboard to find an old rubber bone which he and Blaze used for a game of toss-and-fetch. As dog and boy raced for the door, his mother called to him:

"No, Peter, not today!"

"Aw, Mom! I'm going to stay in the yard!"

"No, Peter, In the house."

"Why, it's nice weather. Does he have a virus?" asked his grandmother.

"He has a little problem that is keeping him indoors." replied her daughter.

Mrs. Robbins looked surprised. Peter scowled. Mumbling something under his breath, he stomped upstairs followed by Blaze. Amy was delighted to have her grandmother as a house guest. She brought her favorite OZ book from her room and politely asked her grandmother to read to her.

"*If* you feel like reading to her, go ahead. I'm about to start dinner. It will be very simple tonight and earlier than usual."

"Can't I help you?" offered Grandmother; but Martha pointed to the comfortable old sofa and turned on a lamp.

"Sit here, Mother. And Amy, don't wear your Grandmother out."

"Goodness, Martha! I'm not that old and feeble," laughed Mrs. Robbins, as she opened the book and began to read.

Meanwhile, upstairs Blaze was playing tug of war with the hem of Peter's jeans. Occasional thumps were heard below. Blaze was given her name because of a white pennant-shaped mark on the right side of her shiny black saddle. She adored the children as they did her.

After dinner Mr. Landon directed the entire family into the living room. There he briefly explained to Grandmother why they had asked her to visit and to bring Blaze with her.

"Well, I knew something was up as soon as Martha phoned me, but I never thought it was anything like this."

Just then the doorbell rang. Mr. Landon ushered in Chief Johnson and Detective Jones. After polite introductions to Mrs. Robbins, the men turned to the children.

"Tell us everything you remember about this King Gnome person," said Chief Johnson.

"He's the gnome king." corrected Amy. "His name is King Klutch."

Mr. Landon gave his daughter a reproachful look, but Mr. Jones was turning on a recorder to catch every word and no one contradicted Amy.

"Where did you first see this man?" asked the Chief.

"In the gnome kingdom, underground in the Great Forest," Peter took up the response.

"You mean in a cave in Chester Woods?"

"No, not Chester Woods. The Great Forest is what we came to after we slid down a hill and right through a cave."

"Then what?"

"We told you last year. King Klutch was trying to destroy Christmas. He paid these horrible old black widows to make a sticky net to capture Santa Claus and all his dwarfs. But we found the Golden Horn, which the gnomes had stolen and hidden in South Tunnel, and I blew it and all the elves came and captured King Klutch and turned all the black widows into spiders," exclaimed Peter.

"Yes, and then they put King Klutch in jail – or whatever they have there," Amy chimed in.

"And then you came home – magically, I suppose?"

"Santa Clause brought us home on Christmas Eve," replied Amy, innocent of the Chief's sarcasm.

"Now tell me about this man you saw the other night."

"It wasn't a man, exactly. It was King Klutch," replied Peter.

"How did you know that in the dark?"

"The street light was shining right in his face. I recognized him even though he was wearing a cloak over his head and around his body. He had the same mean eyes and funny nose."

"Hmmm! And this is the only time you have ever seen this person or gnome since last year?"

"Yes," said Peter softly, lowering his eyes.

Amy squirmed and spoke up.

"Peter, we did see something like that once before."

"Where and when?" snapped the Chief.

"Oh, Amy!" Peter glared at his sister.

"We rode our bikes to Chester Woods one day last month and we took a different biking trail and we came out to a clearing and there was this great big gigantic rock." Amy gestured with outstretched arms to demonstrate the size. "And when we walked around to the other side of it, there was this thing like Peter told you – only he hid his face in the cloak, and we only saw one eye."

"And then what did you do?"

"We ran to our bikes and jumped on and rode home as fast as we could."

"Did he follow you? Was there a car or van or any other vehicle there?" asked Jones.

Both children shook their heads.

"All right. Now we have something to go on," said the Chief. Detective Jones snapped off the recorder.

"We'll be in touch."

"Gnomes have long hairy ears like dogs," ventured Amy, "and they are very, very, very strong."

The two men turned to gaze at the little girl.

"We finally get something real, and then it turns into a fairy tale!" exclaimed Johnson, shaking his head.

"Oh, gnomes are real," Amy replied with the innocence of a nine year old.

"Well," sighed Jones, "we do have the boot. We've sent the fingerprints — odd as they were — to the Feds, and we should hear from them tomorrow. There could be some kinda cult in those woods — hiding out in a cave, maybe."

"Yeah, well, we'll want to talk to you again. Meantime, keep a watch on the children. Keep your doors and windows locked. We'll be going now, but if anything more happens or you need us, call this number," said the Chief, handing a card to Mr. Landon. The policemen then said good-night and departed.

Mr. Landon turned to his children angrily.

"What is this about you two going to Chester Woods on your bikes?"

"See, I told you," growled Peter under his breath as he kicked his sister's foot.

"Well?"

"We thought maybe we could find the cave that was the entrance to the Great Forest, so we could visit Homer and Grandmother Hollyberry," mumbled Peter.

"After all the trouble you brought on your whole family before — you tried to run away and get lost again?" gasped their Mother.

"No, Momma," said Amy, "we didn't *want* to get lost or run away — just a little visit. You've never believed us, so Peter borrowed the camera to take pictures, so you'd *have* to believe."

Peter groaned aloud. Mrs. Landon began to sob.

"Well, I am shocked!" shouted Mr. Landon. "That you would steal my camera, run away from home — and if you hadn't been scared to death by some old tramp, you might have fallen into some cave and never been found.

"And just what are the police going to think about you now that they know they are dealing with runaways?"

"Oh, Daddy, we weren't running away," sobbed Amy, with trembling lip and tears streaming down her cheeks.

"Of course not," her Grandmother came over and put her arm around the trembling child. "They are both trying to tell you the truth, at least as they see it. You and Martha have allowed this whole affair to upset you. Instead of listening to them, you have insisted they are making up tales."

The children turned gratefully to their grandmother, as both parents looked at each other.

"Perhaps you're right, Mother," said Martha. "But the children must understand they are never to go near Chester Woods again — either alone or with anyone else. And for a time at least — maybe a long time — they must stay in the house after school, until the police find out what is going on."

"Oh, dear, yes," agreed Grandmother. "You may invite your friends in to play games, but no going outdoors."

Peter groaned loudly.

"Do you hear that, young man?" asked his father.

"Yes, sir."

"'I'm going to make some cocoa," said Martha. "We'll have some cookies and hot chocolate to help us relax before bedtime. Now you children must be very careful, as Daddy says, until these problems are resolved."

"Welcome to Windchime Castle," said their jovial rescuer.

Chapter 5
A Visit to the Bank

NOVEMBER PASSED INTO DECEMBER. The trees were bare and occasional light snowfalls covered the town of Dunsdale and surrounding fields and forests with the mystical beauty of winter white.

There were no new sightings of the tramp dressed in a gray hood. The police had conducted a thorough search of Chester Woods, the local authorities having been joined by a posse of volunteers; for by now word had circulated that there were people of some sort hiding out in the heavily wooded state park.

However, nothing unusual had turned up. The great boulder, where the children had encountered the stranger, had been located, and a small cave had been discovered nearby. But except for the remains of a few campfires, nothing else was found. Campfires were not unusual in the park because that section of it was frequently used by hikers and Scouts. There was no evidence of cults or any other people hiding out.

Jones and Johnson had checked shelters, hospitals, boarding houses, alley ways, shops, and Dunsdale's one hotel with a police artist's drawing based on the children's description of King Klutch. No one had recognized the picture. They had visited the ticket office at the railroad and bus stations and the car rental agencies, to no avail.

The fingerprint report had caused something of a stir. The prints on the boot were so different from anything on record that the F.B.I. sent two agents to interview Peter and Amy. The children answered all the questions they were asked, and the men left, tight-lipped. Mr. and Mrs. Landon became more and more concerned, since the authorities were taking seriously what they had regarded as childish nonsense.

However, as time passed and Christmas came and went, there were no new events or evidence connected with the mysterious stranger. The police decided to close the case with the conclusion that there was someone who the children thought resembled a person they had reason to fear; but whoever he was, he was long gone from Dunsdale.

Everyone relaxed to a degree. The children were allowed to play outdoors again and to enjoy the winter skating and sledding with friends. Grandmother and Blaze stayed on as extra guardians when Martha found it necessary to be away from home.

So the school year wore on into March. One Saturday morning at breakfast Mrs. Landon said to her children:

"Today we're going shopping for some new spring clothes. You have both grown so much, you'll never fit into last year's things."

"Aw, Mom," protested Peter, "I'm supposed to meet the guys in the school yard for baseball practice!"

"Not this morning, young man. You need new shoes, not to mention summer shirts and jeans. Your socks are in holes, too."

Peter grumbled, but gave in, and soon the three were driving down Main Street in the family car.

"First I have to stop at the bank to cash a check," explained Martha, as she pulled into the parking lot.

"We'll wait here," said Peter; but his mother shook her head. She was still nervous about leaving the children alone in public places.

"No, Peter, we'll all go in together."

Amy hopped out of the car, while Peter followed somewhat reluctantly, and the three entered the First National Bank of Dunsdale. They took their places in the usual long Saturday morning line that curved back upon itself like a serpent before the row of busy tellers. As they neared the front of the line, a door to an office marked Assistant Manager opened and a short stocky man with thick black hair strode out. He was neatly dressed in a gray business suit. There was nothing about his appearance that would arouse the alarm or curiosity of anyone in the bank, but Amy grabbed her mother's arm and whispered,

"There's King Klutch!"

"That's *him*, Mom," agreed Peter. "He's working right here in this bank."

The man in the gray suit looked sharply at the children, and scowling darkly, retreated behind the closed door. Mrs. Landon was stunned by the children's reaction and obvious terror.

"Let's *go!*" implored Peter.

Their turn had come up in the line.

"Wait a minute, Peter. Let me cash this check."

"Is something wrong?" asked the pleasant voice of the teller.

"Who is that man who just came through that door and went back into his office again?"

"Him? That's Mr. Cruekette, our new assistant manager."

"How long has he worked here?"

"I believe he's been here about a month. He isn't very friendly. I really don't know anything about him. Would you like to speak to the manager?"

"Just cash this check for me, please."

"Is anything wrong?" she asked, as she passed the bills under the window.

"No, certainly not, thank you. Come children, we must be on our way."

The children were so distraught that their mother decided to cancel the shopping trip and instead to drive to her husband's office. Mr. Landon, who was naturally quite surprised at their unexpected visit, laid aside his work to give them his full attention. After listening to their account, his face expressed his concern.

"He certainly was, well — rather odd looking," said his wife, "but he was a human being."

"No, he *wasn't*," Amy declared. "He's a gnome!"

"Where were the long hairy ears?" asked her father. "You say he had thick black hair."

"And *long*," chimed in Peter.

"Yes, recalled Martha. "In fact, it was so long we didn't see his ears at all." A shiver of fear went through her.

"Now before we all jump to the wrong conclusions, let's be very calm about this. Martha, instead of going shopping, take the children home and keep them indoors. I'll call Chief Johnson at once and report this, if you are both absolutely sure this man is the tramp you saw."

"We're sure it is King Klutch," the children said together.

"He was a mean looking character," agreed their Mother.

"Mean he may be, but if he isn't this 'King Klutch' we'll all look very foolish indeed."

"Dad, you've got to believe. It *is* King Klutch!"

"Well, we'll see," said his father, as he rose and gave them all a hug. "Now go home, and I shall contact the police and let them decide who this man is."

Chapter 6
An Appointment Kept

THE TWO POLICE OFFICERS CAME TO THE LANDON'S HOUSE that evening. After the usual polite greetings, Chief Johnson announced:

"We've done a routine check of Mr. Cruekette's background. According to the bank's personnel director, he came from Texas, where he was president of a savings and loan company for twenty years until it failed a year ago. He has no criminal record that we can locate. He's doing well on this job — is a genius with the computer, it seems."

"The dude isn't very friendly — he isn't cool — but he does his job okay, so there's no complaint about him," added Erasmus Jones.

"What about the fingerprints?" asked Peter.

"We don't have any of his. We can't go around fingerprinting people, unless there's cause for arrest. As far as we know, this man is not a suspect of any crime — not even vagrancy."

"Yeah, even if he is the tramp by the rock, like you say, he isn't a criminal," added Jones. "He's never made a move to hurt you. We can't arrest a guy for lookin' mean."

"We'll watch him, don't worry," Chief Johnson assured them, "and you watch the children. They disappeared a year and a half ago, and we don't want any repetition of that."

Amy and Peter were so distressed by the thought of having the gnome king living right in their own town that they found it very difficult to concentrate on their school work. As a result, their

31

grades began to drop. They had trouble falling asleep at night and often awoke from wild nightmares of the gnome kingdom.

In these dreams King Klutch and the gnomes were battling Santa Claus and the dwarfs and elves. Occasionally Homer and Mistress Mousie and Grandmother Hollyberry would appear. Then they would have trouble falling asleep again, and in the morning they would feel both dull and weary.

After a few weeks of this, Martha and John decided to take the children to their doctor. They were always too embarrassed to discuss any of this with anyone outside of the family, as if the children's problems were some kind of disgraceful thing, simply unacceptable to both of them. Nevertheless, they made an appointment and on the assigned day they drove to the Medical Building and entered the door marked Dr. D. E. Merritt, Family Practice.

Dr. Merritt, a white haired, pink cheeked, rotund gentleman of seventy, listened intently to the children's account of their adventures, which began with their family picnic in Chester Woods a year and a half ago, right up to their seeing King Klutch in the bank. At the end of their tale, Dr. Merritt chuckled.

"These children have some imagination! Ha, ha, ha! Now, Peter and Amy, you know this isn't real. Make-believe is a part of childhood, but you two are carrying things a little too far!"

"No, no, Dr. Merritt," said Amy, her lip beginning to tremble and tears welling up in her eyes. "It isn't make-believe — it all really happened. We wouldn't go on pretending if it wasn't true. We don't like being kept indoors and watched all the time. And the other kids think we're weird."

"Hmmmm! Well, we'll just have to do something about that then." Turning to the Landons he continued:

"Whatever happened to them those days they were missing has obviously caused this unfortunate condition. It is possible that what occurred during that period was so horrible — so terrifying

— that their minds have simply blocked out the facts and have invented all this fairy tale nonsense to cover it up."

He reached into his desk drawer and took out a pad. After writing on it, he tore off the sheet and handed it to Martha.

"I would suggest that you make an appointment with Dr. Ewell Chew. He has been very successful with war veterans and crime victims who have suffered from similar problems. He treats them with drugs and hypnosis and often gets to the bottom of the trouble. Of course," he added, "you may have to leave them in his private hospital for a few weeks or even months."

Peter and Amy's fear expressed itself in their eyes. "Oh dear!" Martha Landon wept into her handkerchief, and her husband looked stunned.

"If you wish," the doctor continued, "I can set up an appointment for you. I think Dr. Chew would want to see you two first for an interview and a few tests. Then he would meet with the children at a later appointment."

"No, Mom," whispered Peter, pulling at his mother's sleeve; but John Landon nodded his head.

"If it is what you say, the sooner we resolve this problem, the better — for the well-being of the children — for all of us, in fact."

"That is the right attitude, John," said Dr. Merritt, as he rose and shook hands with Martha and John. "Now, Peter and Amy, don't worry your little heads about this any more. In a short while you'll be all well again. No more nightmares or wild imagining, eh?" He reached out to take their hands, but the children put their hands behind their backs.

"Ah, stubborn, eh? Afraid we're going to ruin your little game? You know, they have been getting a lot of attention from this thing — a lot of excitement — while you two have been fretting yourselves to death. Well, my short friends, what do you say about that?"

Both children drew in their lips tightly.

"Ha, ha," laughed Dr. Merritt, as he patted their heads. "We'll be in touch."

He then bade them good day and showed them out of his office.

Chapter 7
Kidnapped

MR. AND MRS. LANDON DISCUSSED THE RESULTS of their visit to the doctor with Grandmother Robbins, but she just shook her head and frowned. Nevertheless, Mr. Landon made an appointment with Dr. Ewell Chew for the following Thursday at 8 p.m. On this very day, quite unexpectedly, a telephone call came in the early afternoon from Mrs. Robbins' niece in Philadelphia. Mrs. Robbins' sister, who had been in the hospital for surgery, had improved to the extent that her doctor had decided to send her home the following day. Mrs. Robbins had promised to help care for her sister for a few weeks while she regained her strength.

"I don't think I should go," said Grandmother, as she hung up the phone.

"Mother, of course you should. Aunt Sarah is expecting you, and both she and Mary need you. There is nothing to worry about here. After our visit with Dr. Merritt, we are certain the children are in no danger."

"Well, if you are absolutely certain — I'll call the railroad station and see if I can catch a train to Philly tonight. May I ask a favor? May I leave Blaze here? I'll surely be back in two or three weeks."

"Of course, Mother. We'll be glad to keep her. After all, you have been helping us for over five months. Besides, the children have grown so fond of her, I'm afraid we'll have to get them a puppy when you and she finally do go home."

Grandmother laughed. "It's the other way around, too. Blaze and I will miss them."

Mrs. Robbins left in a taxi at 5 p.m. She kissed the children good-bye and warned them to stay close to home and to keep away from strangers and automobiles. She was not as confident of their safety as were their parents.

After dinner Martha and John prepared to leave for the interview.

"I don't think we should both go and leave the children here alone," said Martha, her face expressing her anxiety.

"Of course we should! It is all in the children's heads. We must break this circle of fear that has enclosed us before it breaks us. Blaze is here. The phone number of the police department is right there on the telephone table. We will lock the doors with our keys. The children can slide the inside bolts, and they will be perfectly safe. We all must regain our sense of security — our sanity, if you will," exclaimed Mr. Landon rather dramatically. "Dr. Chew says he will begin working with the children after school closes. We'll have to forego our vacation this year, but it will be worth it to get them straightened out and our lives back to normal again."

Martha sighed. Their lives had been so pleasant — so placid — before that picnic in Chester Woods. Now everything was topsy turvy. She watched the tension and the anxiety in the faces of her children and wondered if anything would be normal again.

Peter and Amy sat at opposite sides of the kitchen table, their books and homework spread out before them. They watched their mother and father leave. Peter rose from his chair and slid the heavy bolt across the kitchen door. The shades were drawn and the front door was securely locked.

"Nobody could possibly get in," Peter said, half to Amy and half to reassure himself.

"Peter, we're in terrible trouble," said his younger sister as her eyes began to fill with tears. "I don't want to see that Dr. Ewell Chew or take drugs and stay in his old hospital for our summer vacation."

"I know. It's pretty gross. We could run away, I guess."

"Where would we go? If we went to Uncle Jim and Aunt Dolly's, they'd call Mom and Dad and back we'd come, and everything would be even worse for us."

"No, we can't go to anyone in the family — except maybe Grandmom. You know, I think she's on our side. She just frowned and shook her head when Mom told her about that visit to Dr. Merritt. Maybe she'd run away with us, and we could hide somewhere — in — in — California maybe."

"It would be awful to leave Mother and Daddy," said Amy with a sob.

"Yeah, but what's our choice? We're not crazy, but they're so upset they don't know what to believe; and one thing's sure, they don't believe us."

"Let's talk to Grandmom when she comes back. At least she'll listen to us. And maybe she can think of something to do."

Their conversation was suddenly interrupted by the sound of an automobile pulling into the driveway. Both children ran to the living room window and peered into the twilight. There were no headlights and it was too dark to see who might be in the car.

"Let's call the police!" gasped Amy.

Blaze, who had been dozing in her basket beside the stove, leaped up snarling and barking and made a rush for the kitchen door. At the same moment, someone on the outside turned the knob and pushed the door with such force that the locks and hinges and even the wooden doorframe gave way and the entire door was shoved into the kitchen. The children looked aghast at the fearsome visage of King Klutch himself.

Only Blaze sprang into action. With one long angled leap she closed her teeth on the gnome king's right wrist. Klutch gave a terrible howl, but at the same time reached for the little dog's head with his huge left hand. He forced open Blaze's jaws and extracted his bleeding wrist, then quick as a flash he snatched both of the beagle's floppy ears and held her dangling before the children.

Then there were howls in unimaginable tones, as Blaze reacted to both the pain and the indignity; but the little dog was helpless as she hung wriggling in the air.

"Har, har, har," laughed Klutch. "Look-it what I got!" He didn't appear to notice his bleeding wrist.

"Put Blaze down this minute," cried Amy, stamping her foot, as anger overcame terror. Meanwhile, Peter was quietly sidling over to the telephone. But Klutch saw him from the corner of his eye.

"Halt!" he shouted, "or I'll slam your dog into the wall and break every bone in its body. Aha! That did it! You like your little doggie, eh?"

Blaze continued to howl, making such bellows that the children hoped a neighbor might hear and come to investigate.

"Don't you dare hurt Blaze," cried Amy; "she belongs to Grandmother."

"Oh really? Well, now, I'll tell you what we'll do. We'll lock the nice little doggie in the pantry, but first you fetch some cord or rope, so we can tie her loud mouth shut. And if you make one move to run away, I'll kill her."

With trembling hands, Peter unsuccessfully searched his pocket for a piece of string.

"Get that!" Klutch nodded toward a linen towel hanging by the sink. "Now twist it — like that — fine. Now give it to me."

He tucked Blaze's body tightly under one arm, and with his two free hands held the dog's mouth shut.

"Now tie that towel around her nose and mouth. Tighter. Hurry up."

"She has to breathe," objected Amy.

The little dog was still struggling when the knot was pulled tight, but Klutch tossed her into the pantry and slammed the door.

"You two are taking a ride with me. Remember, one sound out of you and the beast dies!"

He grasped Amy's upper arm and Peter's hair in a vice-like grip and marched them through the open door.

38

However, the noise of breaking down the door along with Blaze's howls had been overheard by the neighbors who lived next door.

"What's all the racket?" inquired Mr. Blakeley, laying down his newspaper and pipe.

"Can't imagine," his wife replied. She was knitting a sweater and had reached the part of counting stitches, and didn't welcome anything that would break her concentration. Besides, all sorts of speculations had been circulating about the Landon family. Since Mr. and Mrs. Landon had given no explanation to anyone for fear people would think them crazy at the very least, rumors began to fly around that they were in some kind of terrible trouble with either mobsters or drug dealers who were threatening their children. Mr. Blakeley went to the window and peered through the curtain.

"Hmmm, that's odd. The Landon's white Ford is gone, but there is a strange dark car in their driveway. Can't see much of it through the hedge, through. Appears the driver backed it in. Maybe I should go next door and see if those kids are okay."

"No, no, Harry," implored his wife. "They might have guns!"

"Well, we can't just ignore this. Listen! Listen to that dog! I'll give them a call." He left the window and walked over to the telephone table.

"Everything has quieted down," said Mrs. Blakeley.

Her husband picked up the receiver and dialed his neighbor's number. After letting it ring for several minutes, he hung up.

"I don't like it. I don't like it one bit."

At that instant they heard the sound of a car starting. He rushed to the window in time to see the dark automobile pull quickly out of the Landon's driveway, turn right on Maple Avenue and speed away.

Mr. Blakeley ran back to the telephone and dialed 911.

Peter and Amy climbed upon Rondo's back for the long journey to the Gingerbread Inn.

Chapter 8
The Secret Cavern

KING KLUTCH SHOVED THE CHILDREN INTO THE REAR OF THE CAR and hopped into the driver's seat. An instant later he had turned on the ignition, locked the doors, and shifted into drive. They were rolling down the street the next minute, and had soon left the town behind. Klutch was careful not to exceed the speed limit or do anything else that might attract attention.

The rosy glow of the spring sunset had faded from the sky, which was now a dull blue-gray. The moon had not yet risen and the stars were veiled by a thin spring mist. Once they had passed the boundaries of Dunsdale, there was little traffic as they headed toward Chester Woods along the state highway. At last Klutch pulled into a narrow unpaved road that led into a dark, dense section of the forest. As the road narrowed to little more than a trail, the car bumped along over roots and rocks up a steep hill.

Tree limbs struck the windshield and scraped the sides and roof of the car. Peter quietly searched about on the floor, hoping to find some tool — a wrench or hammer perhaps — that he could use as a weapon; but there was nothing there. At last they reached the crest of a hill. Klutch left the road and pulled over beside a deep ravine. He turned off the ignition and applied the brake.

"Get out!" he ordered, "and don't make one move to run away."

As Peter and Amy started to make a dash into the dark woods, he sprang with the agility of a cat and again grabbed Peter by his hair and Amy by her arm. He was unbelievably strong. As he dragged them down into the ravine, Peter stealthily unbuckled his belt and rolled it up as he slipped it through the loops of his

41

trousers. In the dark Klutch didn't notice. They finally paused at the bottom of the ravine where they saw a dark hole, which proved to be a narrow, low entrance to a cave.

"Crawl in!" ordered Klutch.

The children had no choice but to obey; but as he knelt down, Peter shoved his belt into a clump of wild blueberry bushes that grew beside the opening. They were both so terrified they couldn't speak or even feel the pain from Klutch's grip on them. Klutch was somewhat breathless himself, however, but he managed to light an ancient oil lamp which hung from a rocky projection, and shove a heavy boulder into the entrance of the cave. Then he sat down to rest and surveyed the children.

Finally Peter found his voice and his courage.

"What do you think you're doing? The police and the F.B.I. are going to close in on you, just as soon as Mom and Dad get home from their appointment."

Klutch laughed.

"That is not likely to happen, my *dear, dear* children," he sneered. "The headline news tomorrow morning is not going to be about you. It will be about the collapse of the First National Bank of Dunsdale. I have robbed them of $151 million dollars and everything of value from the safe deposit boxes. Oh! ha, ha! hee, hee, har! They'll find out tomorrow! My only regret is that I won't be there to see it all. Oh, what a blast! What fun! How delicious!"

"What! How could you do that?" gasped Peter.

"It is very easy if one knows how. You dig tunnels and you manipulate. I learned how to work computers in three days. They called me a 'genius,' whatever that means. It was easy to rob the gnomes in my kingdom and make them work their lives away, digging up more and more treasure for me. The poor fools were actually happy to work, even though I allowed them to keep very little." He paused to grin at the children.

"I'm really not bad, not bad at all. I wanted to enslave the dwarfs so they could do the dangerous work instead of my own people. You see, I really *care* about my people.

"That evil gang of elves, with Santa Claus and Elfin and YOU — " he paused to scowl darkly at the children — "along with that incredible cat and Grandmother Hollyberry, de-throned me and threw me into a prison." As he said all this, his countenance took on such a dark, evil expression, so filled with hatred, that the children stared at him in amazement and fear.

"Well, a king does not fall so easily to such a scruffy lot! I tunneled out of the cell. It was purely chance that my tunnel led to this forest. Once I realized I was free and in your dimension, I planned revenge. I discovered your underworld and got fake I.D. Your monetary system and computers were easy for me to understand and manipulate.

"If you two had obeyed your parents and never come here on your bikes that day, you'd be safe in your beds now. But you didn't, did you? So here you are and here you'll stay, so you will never be able to identify me. All my stolen treasure is hidden in another cave. Originally I had planned to kidnap you and hold you for ransom, until I found that your parents are worth very little — financially dwarfs, in fact. So I used fake references to get myself hired by the bank, where I could gather up some *real* wealth." His eyes shone with a combination of greed and glee.

"And do you know what I am going to do now? I am going to gather up my sacks of treasures from the other cave and walk down a new tunnel which I have already dug right into the Valley of the Trolls. I will hire them and form a new army to attack the creatures of the Great Forest, and this time I'll destroy them all!" he shouted with a wild gleam in his eyes.

"Then I'll take back my kingdom of gnomes and grow richer...and richer...and richer..." Klutch was kneeling before the children with his face close to theirs.

"What about us?" asked Peter.

Klutch chuckled. "You must be punished for trying to fight the king. You are hereby sentenced to stay in this cave until you starve to death. They'll never find you here!"

Amy began to sob, but Peter in a rush of desperation reached forward and grabbed Klutch's hair. The king jumped to his feet as the wig came off in Peter's hand. Klutch stood before them with his pointed furry ears securely taped down to his head, looking quite ridiculous. In spite of their danger, Peter and Amy laughed.

White with rage at this indignity, Klutch lunged toward Peter, who adroitly side-stepped the attacker. Thrown off balance, Klutch pitched head first into the rocky wall of the cave and lay on the ground, momentarily stunned.

"Quick!" cried Peter grabbing the lantern, "we have to get out of here!"

They ran to the other side of the cavern, hunting for an opening in the rock. As they searched, Klutch began to recover himself, and holding his battered head in his right hand, he lunged foreword to grab Peter with his left.

"You dare to treat a king like that? For that you die! die! die!"

The children shrank in terror against the rocky wall as the reeling gnome drew nearer. Suddenly there was a strange motion in the cave. The floor began to sway and roll beneath their feet, and rocks began to rain down around them. Then a section of the wall collapsed and buried Klutch in a pile of rubble. Behind what had appeared to be a solid wall of rock, they saw the opening of a tunnel.

Peter snatched Amy's hand. "Come on," he cried, as he squeezed the lantern and himself behind the fallen rock and dragged Any with him.

"Oh, Peter," wailed Amy, "we can't leave him here buried alive." But Peter pulled Amy on.

"It must be an earthquake. We have to get out of here," gasped Peter as stones and soil rained down around them.

Before they had walked more than ten feet along the tunnel, the motion of the earth subsided. The entire quake has lasted less than a minute. The children hurried on without looking back.

Chapter 9
Escape

PETER AND AMY STUMBLED THROUGH THE RUBBLE that littered the floor of the tunnel. In addition to the rocks, there were fissures in the ground, one so wide that they had to leap over it. There were boulders so large blocking the tunnel that they had to squeeze past them or climb over. Peter feared they would come to a place where the passage was totally blocked, or the lantern would burn out, or even worse that there would be another earthquake. He remembered reading that earthquakes were usually followed by aftershocks. He didn't express any of these thoughts aloud, because Amy was already so distraught she could hardly keep going.

They must have struggled along for half a mile when the wick sputtered and the light went out. Amy began to sob. Peter set down the lantern and put his arm around his little sister.

"Don't give up, Amy. We've made it this far. You stay here. Before the light went out I saw what looked like a turn just ahead. I want to see if I was right and feel my way around it to find out what may be there."

"Please don't leave me, Peter."

"Just for a few minutes. You stay right here and don't move. I'll be right back."

In spite of Amy's sobbing protests, Peter felt his way carefully along the wall. He tested each step ahead, for fear he might fall into a fissure. But the floor of the tunnel now was solid rock and seemed to be clear of rubble, as if there had been no earthquake here at all.

At last he reached the place he had dimly glimpsed, where the wall on his left ended and the tunnel took a sharp right angle turn.

He felt his way around the rocky corner, gingerly placing one foot before the other. Suddenly there was no longer total darkness. A hazy light was coming in far ahead and dimly illuminating the floor of the tunnel. He walked cautiously forward. The tunnel was widening as he neared the light, and he realized that he was approaching an opening. Stooping low, he emerged onto a rocky ledge. The light which now seemed so bright to his eyes was that of the stars and a full moon.

He took a few gulps of the sweet pine-scented air and saying a silent prayer of thanks in his heart, hurried back into the tunnel to where Amy crouched huddled against the wall. The moonlight had been so bright that the tunnel seemed darker than before, so that he bumped into her before he saw her.

"Oh, Peter, thank goodness you're back!"

"Amy, we're saved. The end of the tunnel is just a few hundred feet around the bend. Come on! Let's get out while the moon is still up to light the way."

Feeling their way carefully, they were soon out of the darkness and were standing upon a wide ledge of smooth rock. Below them the ground fell away, as if they were on the side of a mountain. Tops of conifers, clearly defined in the moonlight, pierced a veil of mist, below which they could see nothing.

"We'll have to stay here for the night," said Peter.

"It's cold," said Amy shivering.

"We'll huddle up close to keep warm. We've made it this far — we'll be all right. The sun is sure to rise sometime, and after all, it is April."

Chapter 10
A Visit To Windchime Castle

I T WAS A LONG, LONG NIGHT FOR PETER AND AMY, waiting for dawn
at the mouth of the tunnel. They did not express to one
another their shared fears of wild animals or the recurrence
of an earthquake, nor what problems and dangers might confront
them the following day when the rising sun would reveal their
surroundings.

At last, however, the morning star appeared like a fairy god-
mother in a dark sky that was beginning to glow with a blue light
in the east. They watched as the rising light turned the sky into a
rosy gold. Then a rim of fire appeared above the mountains in the
distance. The sun rose swiftly and the light of morning flooded the
landscape. Amy, seeing her first sunrise, was awestruck by the
beauty of the scene. Now they could view their surroundings and
comprehend where they were.

The wide ledge upon which they were standing appeared to be
protruding from the side of a mountain. Below they could see the
tops of budding trees mingling with stately conifers which covered the lower slopes. The valley was still shrouded in the early
morning mist, but miles distant on the opposite side of the valley
another mountain range rose in majestic splendor. As the sun
climbed higher in the east, a light spring breeze also picked up,
and somewhere off in the distance the children heard a tinkling of
musical notes.

"Do you hear that?" asked Amy.

"Yep," agreed her brother, glancing up expecting to see the
mountain rising above him. Instead he saw a wooden platform
about fifteen feet above their heads, protruding over the rock
ledge where they were standing. The platform was braced by stout

beams built into the side of the slope; and judging from the appearance of the wood, it had been there a long, long time.

"Look!" exclaimed Peter. "Great jumping beans! What's that?"

"There must be people around. Maybe if we yell for help they'll hear us."

"Wait a minute. We may not want whatever is up there to hear us. Let's see if there is a path up or down the mountain first."

They explored the ground around the ledge, but found no sign of a trail. On both sides and below them there was a steep dropoff. The steep rock strewn slopes had only clumps of tough grasses, nothing that one could trust as a footing or handhold.

"Well," decided Peter, "it looks as if the only way out of here is up, and we will need help to get there. We'll have to take our chances and yell."

So both children shouted for help as loudly as they could, but the only reply was the sound of the wind. After they had shouted until they were hoarse, a number of birds fluttered by. Some of them perched on the ledge close to the children and regarded them with cocked heads and bold bright eyes. The birds seemed to converse with one another in their own language, which went something like this:

"Swing-it, swing-it, swing-it, swing-it!"

The red bird sang, "Pretty, pretty, pretty, pretty."

"Chippee, chippee, chippee, cheek," another called.

Then the three birds engaged in what appeared to be an argument.

"Ahh-weechi, weechi, weechi, weechi!"

"Receeder, receeder, receeder rist!" screamed another with an annoyed flutter of its wings.

"Cheater, cheater, cheater, cheater!" cried the red bird as he flew around the children's heads and out of sight.

"Oh, bother!" cried Peter, annoyed by these audacious, squabbling creatures.

"Tea too, tea too, tea too!" sang another bird, and then they all flew away.

"Well, weren't they the nerviest birds you ever saw!" cried Amy. "They were so big and bold."

"Yes," agreed Peter, "they didn't seem to be one bit afraid of us. It looks as if the only way we'll ever get off this ledge is to braid some of this tough grass into a rope so we can let ourselves down the mountain."

The children began pulling all the grass they could reach. The soil was dry and loose, so the clumps came up fairly easily. When they had made a large pile of the tough blades, they began braiding the grasses and tying the ends together. Peter was thankful for his Boy Scout training in tying knots. They had been working over an hour when they heard a scraping, creaking sound on the platform overhead. As they looked up, a trapdoor opened and a round rosy face looked down at them.

"Goodness gracious! However did you children get down there?" asked a deep friendly voice.

"We'll tell you if you help us get off this ledge," replied Peter.

"Yes indeedy, indeedy! Let me see, we'll need the rope ladder I guess. Hasn't been used for several centuries. Hope it hasn't rotted from the dampness of those valley mists. Now just you wait there for a few minutes and don't go near the edge." He closed the trap door.

In a very short time, which seemed like a very long time to the children, the trap door was reopened, and they could see a bundle of rope being fastened to two posts. The stranger then let down the ladder until the bottom rung was resting on the rocky ledge.

"Now climb up very carefully. Hold on tightly and take your time. Let the little girl come first. There, that's fine."

As Amy reached the top rung, a large hand and arm was thrust through the hole, and Amy was pulled to safety.

"Come on, Peter," she called, "it's all right."

Peter lost no time climbing the ladder and soon was standing beside his sister on a wide, deep platform enjoying a spectacular view of the surrounding mountains.

"Welcome to Windchime Castle," said their jovial rotund rescuer, who was wearing a suit of purple velvet embroidered with gold threads. He had a short white beard and bushy white eye-brows beneath which sparkled very bright blue eyes. "How long have you children been on the ledge?"

"Just last night and this morning," replied Amy.

"Let us climb up to my castle and breakfast together while you tell me all about yourselves — where you have come from and how you happened to visit Windchime Castle."

He pointed to a long, steep stairway cut into the rock of the mountain, which led straight upward to a gray granite castle that seemed to rise right out of the mountain itself. Amy felt dizzy from the great height, while Peter had some misgivings from the austere appearance of the castle; but they really had no choice except to go up the steps. Since their host seemed amiable enough, they turned to ascend the long, steep flight of granite steps.

Chapter 11
Elfberries

AS THEY CLIMBED THE STEEP STAIRWAY, the children began to hear ripples of musical notes, some light and tinkly and others deeper and beautifully harmonic. At the top of the stairs was a wide patio made of the native rock. The castle loomed overhead, so high that they had to tip their heads as far back as possible to see the turrets from which flew pennants of gold, scarlet, and purple. Windchimes also danced from the turrets and the overhang of balconies.

When they had reached the top step, they found themselves facing a wide oaken door, so heavy that it was a great effort for the doorman to push it open. They entered a hall paved in green marble. After climbing another marble stairway to a wide foyer, they arrived at a cheerful sunlit room. Here a table was laden with fruit and sweet rolls piled high on a silver platter.

"Sit down now and let us eat together while you tell me how you happened to be on that ledge," their host said.

Peter and Amy, dirty and exhausted from the terrifying night before and the long climb up the stairways, sank gratefully into the comfortable chairs and watched the servants bring in a pitcher of fresh milk and a steaming pot of something that had a vaguely familiar fragrance.

"How did you know we were on the ledge?" asked Peter. "Did you hear us call for help?" He wondered how anyone so far up the mountain and inside a stone castle could have heard their cries over the sound of all the windchimes.

"Dear me, no, laddie. My birds were on a morning flight to breakfast on the elfberries that grow on the mountain slopes in the spring. They saw you and flew into my window to tell me of your predicament. I rushed from the castle and down the steps as

51

fast as I could, for I feared you might try to climb up or down the mountain, which would be extremely dangerous at that slope."

"Your *birds* told you?" exclaimed Amy.

"Ah, yes, we receive many messages from the birds and also from the wind."

"Where are we?" asked Amy. She thought it would be rather rude to say "Who are you?"

"You are, as I believe I said, at Windchime Castle. I am Duke Ron de Lay, ruler of Granite Mountain and scientific investigator. And may I ask who you are?"

"We're Amy and Peter Landon," Peter replied.

"Peter and Amy? Did you ever visit the Great Forest before?"

"Yes," replied Amy, "and we are here because King Klutch escaped from prison and tunneled right into our State Park."

"We saw him," Peter took up the tale, "but we couldn't make anyone believe us when we told them who he was."

"Yes, and he got a job at our bank and he saw us and he remembered who we were and he broke into our house when Mother and Daddy were out and he made us get into a car with him because Grandmom had to go to Philadelphia to take care of Aunt Sarah, and he drove us to that park again and dragged us into a cave and the earthquake came and a wall fell down and we ran down the tunnel." Amy finally stopped for breath.

Duke Ron de Lay was leaning forward in fascination.

"You mean to tell me that you are the two children who helped to save Santa Claus and the dwarfs from the gnomes a year and a half ago?"

"Yes!" both children replied together.

"How marvelous! I am delighted to meet you. You have already become subjects of song and stories here. And to think that I have had this very morning the privilege of rescuing *you!*" He reached across the table and shook the children's hands. "Do you realize you are the only mortals who have ever returned to the Great Forest?"

"Is that where we really are?" asked Amy.

"Windchime Castle is at the western edge of the Great Forest. This afternoon I shall take you to my laboratory where we record the messages the windchimes bring us."

"What sort of messages?" asked Amy.

"News of everything that is happening in the Great Forest. Every sound is carried on the wind, you know. Most of the time you hear the wind as a rushing through leaves of trees, or the sighing of pines, or a howling around the house. But actually every sound that is made, every spoken word or note sung, every sound of beast or bird is borne on the wind. When that wind reaches my windchimes, they play. Their music is then recorded by a special machine.

"Another machine translates these recordings back into what they were when they were originally uttered. Thus I can learn everything our people or animals are saying or doing."

"Do you mean you understand the language of cats and dogs and birds?" asked Peter in amazement.

"Some of it, dear boy, some of it. But after all, who understands everything that others are saying to them, even when they are speaking the same language?"

"That is certainly true," replied Peter thoughtfully.

"Yes," agreed Amy, "our mother and father didn't understand what we were trying to tell them."

"So I learn a great deal from my study of the winds and the sounds of animals and birds. My students are constantly involved in research. We are learning more and more each day."

"So here we are again in the Great Forest, and we're drinking elf flower tea!"

"Right you are, little lady. Do eat heartily, because you have had a frightful experience. But you are now safe. After breakfast you may want to wash and put on fresh clothing. We don't have clothes like yours here, but there are other garments that I have ordered for you waiting in your rooms. Enjoy your morning resting or browsing around the castle and gardens. There is much for you to explore.

"We'll lunch here when the sun shines through the south window. Afterwards we'll go out on a balcony overlooking the countryside, and I'll show you exactly where you are."

Amy and Peter were happy to wash away the soil from the tunnel in the warm water of a marble tub that was almost large enough to be called a swimming pool. Everything in Windchime Castle was, like the owner, very large. Their spacious rooms were located on a corner with two French doors that opened onto balconies, providing a view of the magnificent scenery of mountain ranges and the valley below. Sunlight flooded the room, brightened still further by the white walls and furniture, all of which was decorated with gold.

There were two comfortable beds and several chairs and tables. The clothes laid upon the beds were quite different from what the children normally wore, but everything fit them well and was comfortable. Peter surveyed himself before a long mirror.

"The guys would really laugh at me in this outfit," he chuckled, admiring himself in the blue velvet knee britches, a pale yellow silk shirt, and a tunic of deep rose.

"You really do look gorgeous, Peter," agreed Amy.

"So do you," replied her brother as he observed his sister in a pale green organdie dress embroidered with pink and white roses. "Our folks wouldn't recognize us if they could see us like this. We're different people, and I like the difference."

"Well, here we are again on a wonderful adventure in the Great Forest, and Mom and Dad aren't going to believe this one either, I'll bet," said Amy.

"Yeah. I wonder what they're doing now?"

"Probably worrying themselves to death. If they had just listened to us when we tried to warn them, King Klutch would be in jail and none of this would have happened."

"Then we'd never have returned."

"That's true," agreed Amy. "Grandmother always says that everything always happens for a purpose. Maybe King Klutch wouldn't be in jail. Maybe he would just have run away and be stealing somewhere else."

"I don't think he'll do any harm now — I hope."

"Unless he can get out of that rock pile and escape from the cave or through the tunnel, like we did."

"We'd better mention that possibility to the Duke," said Peter.

Chapter 12
Duke Ron de Lay

THE CHILDREN PASSED THE MORNING roaming through the castle and the gardens. They visited the dairy and the pottery and even the kitchens, where all manner of delectable foods were being prepared for the great party to honor the visitors. They also met many of the Duke's people, who were friendly and happy like the dwarfs, but tall and slim. Young or old, they were all quite jolly.

When they rejoined the Duke for lunch, Peter spoke of the possibility of the Gnome King's escaping from the rubble and returning to the Great Forest as they had done. Duke Ron de Lay smiled.

"My dear boy, I have already thought of that possibility and have sent some men to seal up the tunnel where it enters the cave. It had been sealed years ago, of course, but the earthquake knocked down the wall we had built.

"The entrance is now sealed up again, but my men found no sign of Klutch in the cave. Rubble was scattered all about the floor, and there was no longer a boulder at the mouth of the cave."

"Then he's escaped again?" gasped Amy.

"Perhaps. He either could have returned to the Great Forest or he may be in your land."

Both children shivered with fright.

"Now, now, you are not to worry. We have posted guards everywhere in case he has followed you through the tunnel. So far no one has seen him. Remember, the cave entrance is open, so he very likely didn't return but made his escape into your — what did you call it? state park?"

"Well, he won't be safe there because we have disappeared, and now the police and the F.B.I. will be looking everywhere for us and for him too."

"Perhaps they won't know where to search for him."

"That's right, Peter," added Amy, "and remember he had a car."

"What is a 'car'?" asked the Duke.

The children looked at him in surprise. Peter tried to explain.

"It's like a metal box on four wheels. It has an engine that makes the wheels turn, and there's a steering wheel, so you can drive anywhere you want to go."

"Ah!" replied the Duke, "How ingenious! I must see one of those some day."

"How do you travel here?" inquired Amy.

"We don't travel very often. When we do, we just walk or ride the horses. Actually I have never been away from Granite Mountain. There is so much work to do here in my laboratory that I have never had time to travel."

"You have never been to the North Pole or the Gingerbread Inn?" asked Amy.

"Alas, no, but we keep in touch by messengers and carrier pigeons. Also, the wind chimes, which bring me news of nearly everything that happens in the Great forest. How do you send messages in your country?"

"We telephone. We also have radio and television," replied Peter.

"What are those things like?"

Peter and Amy tried to draw pictures of a telephone, a radio, and a television set and to explain how the messages were carried by wires and ether waves. The Duke found all this very confusing.

"I do know we have satellites way up in outer space that pick up and send back all sorts of information to us," said Peter, "but I don't know exactly how that works." The Duke shook his head in amazement.

"How do you get up and down the mountain?" asked Peter.

"It is possible to do that on secret stairways we have built. But no one wants to venture into the Valley of the Trolls."

"Why not?" asked Peter.

"Their valley is always shrouded in mist, except in the winter when it is covered with ice and deep snow. Then we can see a little more of it. But we never have seen a troll, for they stay in their houses until spring, when the mists return. Nobody knows anything about them, or even what they look like. They stay to themselves and we let them alone."

"Then are you saying we will not be able to visit the Gingerbread Inn?" asked Amy, disappointment showing in her face.

"Well, there is one way that is somewhat dangerous; but if you are willing to take the risk, you could try it. My people use it when it is necessary to visit North Pole, which is located on the summit of the Mountain range that you have already viewed on the opposite side of the valley."

"What way is that?" asked Peter, leaning forward eagerly.

"We have a sturdy basket attached to a pulley. The rope goes from a tower on our mountain to another tower at North Pole. The ropes go right over the Valley of Trolls. As I said, we don't use this very often because of the danger of upsetting; but we regard it as a safer mode of travel than sending our people into the valley to face dangers we know not of. It is, of course, the unknown dangers that are the most terrifying."

"What you need is a helicopter," said Amy.

"A what did you say?"

"A whirlybird," replied Peter. Then seeing how puzzled the Duke was he tried to explain. "It's like a metal box with wings that twirl round and round so fast the box lifts off the ground and flies through the air and takes you wherever you want to go."

"How amazing! Your people do such marvelous things with your magical metal boxes!"

"It isn't magic," said Amy. "We don't have any real magic in America. It just runs by an engine."

"You say you don't have magic? My dear child, I disagree with you. You tell me you fly around in a box which has wings that twirl. That is magic! We have metal boxes, but they never fly. Our birds have wings, but they never twirl; they flap up and down. You have some strange way of getting news from the air, from wires and objects in the sky. We use carrier pigeons or windchimes."

Peter and Amy were thoughtful and quiet for a few minutes.

"Well, maybe we do have magic in a way," said Amy, "but it isn't like elf magic."

"Ah, the elves! Yes, but they are light years ahead of us. We will probably never be like them. But these boxes of yours that go everywhere fascinate me."

"Maybe you could go home with us and study them," suggested Peter.

"That would indeed be delightful, but alas, it is impossible. If I left this dimension and came into yours, assuming I could succeed in doing that, I would die immediately, because I am 539 years old."

The children looked at the duke in amazement.

"Never mind," consoled Amy, "you can get messages from the wind and understand the languages of birds and animals. That is way beyond anything we can do."

"Is that really true, my dear? Then if I am the only one to have accomplished this much, I will know my research has some importance and I have not labored all these years in vain."

"Golly, to understand what birds and animals are saying is super!" said Peter. "That was the problem when we were here before. The mice found out where the gnomes had hidden the Golden Horn and they told the Red Bird who told Homer and the reindeer, but none of the animals could tell Santa or Grandmother Hollyberry."

"So I have heard, and that is why I have pressed on with this research, which has also helped us to understand how much like us these creatures truly are. Now since we have finished lunching, let us visit the laboratory where you can see our various experiments and projects."

Chapter 13
In the Round Tower

PETER AND AMY FOLLOWED DUKE RON DE LAY up a spiral iron stairway which wound round and round and straight up to a breathtaking height until they finally reached the top floor of the highest tower of the castle. Amy felt quite dizzy as she looked over the railing to the floor far below. The Duke took her arm gently.

"Do not be afraid, little one; we will not let you fall. Just step onto the platform and look straight ahead at the door."

Amy felt embarrassed, but she followed the suggestion as the Duke turned the bronze handle and pushed the door open. They entered a vast circular room. Here they saw some of the wondrous machines which the Duke had invented during his many years of scientific research.

There was an ancient loom that wove cloth from yarn spun from clouds and sunlight. Tailors were busy in one area cutting and sewing clothing made from this beautiful lustrous material. Peter and Amy observed that the cloth was of a rather coarse weave, somewhat like burlap, but it was shiny white and silky soft to the touch. It was indeed quite unlike any other material the children had ever seen. Not all the fabric was white, however, for there were huge vats where men were dyeing it various shades of yellow, green, rose, scarlet, purple, and indigo.

Other workers were making hats from a saffron yarn. First the yarn was twisted on a special machine into a thick rope. Then it was coiled round and round forms of various sizes. These coils were carefully stitched together by hand and then removed from the forms. They were lined with stiff material to hold their shape and became the unique hats worn by all the inhabitants of Granite

Mountain. Some were very small to fit the babies while others were large enough for adults because, as the Duke explained, everyone wore the hats for protection from the severe cold of winter, the hot sun of summer, and the winds of all seasons.

The Duke beckoned the children to come with him to another part of the tower. Here there were young men and women clad in the shiny white material who were at work on very strange machines. They were recording readings from some, removing long strips of paper-like tape from others, and then feeding the tapes into other machines.

"These are my assistants," explained the Duke. "Now let us visit Wondo and his group. He is operating a machine that picks up the sounds borne on the winds that blow around this tower and set the windchimes in motion."

Wondo was softly singing to himself; and as they drew near, the children managed to hear some of his song:

"South Wind blows the sweetest breath,
gardenias and roses,
North Wind shrieks around our tower
and tweaks our little noses,
East Wind brings the rain and gales
to gouge the sea and toss the sails,
West Wind brings a sunny day
that dawns and shines and fades away."

Amy thought the song had a sad sound.

"The music of the windchimes is recorded on the tapes from these great spools that you see before you. Then the tape is fed into these machines where the musical notes are unscrambled and restored to their original sounds, which are then recorded and stored in these little boxes," continued the Duke. "Then the boxes are dated and filed in the dungeons of the castle, so they are available at any time.

"Every day I listen to every tape that is made. If there is a problem that threatens anyone in the Great Forest, I immediately dispatch carrier pigeons to the Gingerbread Inn and the North Pole. If the situation is something we can handle, we will take care of it. If it is a major problem, such as — let us suppose — an attack by an army of trolls led by King Klutch, then Grandmother Hollyberry would remove the Golden Horn from Lothra, the most ancient tree in the forest, and blow it to summon the elves. Their magic is powerful enough to control any situation."

"It surely is," agreed Peter. "We saw what they did to old King Klutch and Klutter and Klatter."

"And the Black Widows," added Amy.

"Yes. It would have been far worse for them if Elfin had had his way. But Santa Claus was, as usual, so kind and forgiving that we now have a new problem with Klutch," replied the Duke. "Now let me show you how these machines work. Let us step out upon this balcony."

He led the children through a glass door. They were so high up above the valley, they could almost touch the overhanging clouds. Peter and Amy stood in awe of the beauty of the scene.

"Now," continued the Duke, "here is a cluster of windchimes hanging from the canopy overhead that pick up winds that blow from the north and south. Their music is recorded first on these discs that are spinning here before your eyes. The disks are then put on the machine that produces the tapes, which in turn are fed into the decoding machine that translates all the holes in the tape back into the original sound."

"Wow!" exclaimed Peter.

"The other balcony on the south side of the tower records the east-west winds in the same manner. Those are the chimes most likely to pick up news from the Gingerbread Inn.

"Now here on the rail we have mounted our largest viewing glass. Since it is a clear day, you should be able to see North Pole and Santa's castle — if you will turn this a bit to the northeast — ah, there it is. Have a look yourselves." The Duke was maneuvering the large instrument and adjusting the lens.

Peter stepped up and peered into the glass.

"Great jumping beans! There it is!"

"Let me have a turn, Peter," cried Amy.

"Wait a minute; I haven't finished. There's something red standing on a flat green spot over there — behind the palace."

"Let me see," said the Duke. Peter stepped aside and the Duke peered into the lens. "Ah ha! That is Rondo. He appears to be grazing on some fresh spring grass," he chuckled.

Peter and Amy suddenly had a great desire to revisit all their old friends. Then it was Amy's turn to look.

"I can see some dwarfs," she said. "I think they are cutting trees."

"They could be," agreed the Duke, "perhaps for firewood or even for toys next Christmas."

"You said there is a way we could get to North Pole from here," said Peter.

"Yes there is, and I shall show it to you; but first let us go inside and see what messages have been picked up today."

"Oh, goody, yes!" cried Amy.

They returned to the tower room.

"Here is an interesting item, sir," said Wondo. "It came in via the east-west chimes and has just been decoded. Homer was crying all night. Rosebud, his little son, has disappeared and cannot be found anywhere. This morning he started out to search the entire Great Forest until he finds the kitten. He told all this to Mistress Mousie when they were in the herb garden behind the Inn."

"Does Grandmother Hollyberry know about this?" asked the Duke.

"Unfortunately, he cannot talk to her, and she may still be unaware that the kitten is missing."

"Then she will think something has happened to Homer. We must send a message to her by carrier pigeon at once, and also one to Santa Claus, so everyone in the Great Forest can help search."

"Yes, sir. We'll get it on wing at once."

"Keep me informed, Wondo. And add that Peter and Amy are with me." The Duke smiled at the thought of how surprised and happy his friends would be to hear *his* news.

"Now it is approaching dinner time. Let us leave the tower and prepare to dance and feast," said the rotund Duke. "I am giving a party tonight in your honor. All my people on Granite Mountain have been invited, so they can personally meet the boy and girl who saved Santa Claus."

"Actually it was Homer and the elves who did that," corrected Amy.

"Ah, my dear children, how you underestimate the part you played! It was you, Peter, who overheard the gnomes. If you had not told Grandmother Hollyberry the next day, King Klutch would have succeeded in his evil schemes. We could not have picked anything up with the windchimes because the gnomes live underground, and Klutter and Klatter were talking softly indoors. The blizzard brought on by North Wind further softened any sound.

"Then you both walked through all that snow to North Pole, and you, Peter, blew the horn after Homer dug it up. You are both truly heroes and deserve to be praised in song and story. If you had not been here, we might all be slaves of King Klutch by now."

"That's right," agreed Amy, "but Homer and the red bird and the mice and reindeer did their part too. It's really no wonder Mother and Daddy don't believe us. It's all so strange and wonderful."

"Strange because it is so alien to your world," replied the Duke, "and wonderful because you are the kind of children you are. But now let's return to the lower floors and dress for the banquet this evening."

Willy and Nilly began to work the pulley.
"Take care — hold tight — and God's speed!" the Duke called.

Chapter 14
An Unexpected Mishap

THE PARTY THAT EVENING AT WINDCHIME CASTLE was held in the grand ballroom. Everyone who lived on Granite Mountain was invited and all came, dressed in their very finest costumes. They were eager to see Amy and Peter, whose bravery had saved them from the wicked King Klutch.

Amy was dazzled by the beauty of the inhabitants and their clothing. Most of it was fashioned from the cloth made from clouds and sunlight, which she had seen being woven and dyed in the tower. One of the weavers told her that Ron de Lay had discovered the process two hundred years ago. It had been his first great scientific achievement. The colors were so bright that it was easy to see that one of the components of the material was light.

Other guests wore costumes made from the wool of sheep and goats which shepherds tended on the high pasturelands. Everyone looked elegant. A fire blazed in the massive stone hearth to take the early April chill off the great hall.

Peter and Amy were happy to see that there were other children their own age present, and they lost no time getting acquainted. After the last guest had arrived and been introduced, everyone lined up for the beautiful formal dancing that was the fashion on Granite Mountain. The musicians began to play music that was so sweet and beautiful it made the children light-hearted and happy just to hear it.

After much dancing and singing, the great doors to the banquet hall were thrown open to a fanfare of trumpets. All the guests filed in to take their assigned seats at the tables. The food and drink were so delicious and so elegantly served, that the children thought they must try to remember every detail of the evening as the most special party of their lives.

While they dined, minstrels sang ballads about Peter and Amy and all the others who saved the Great Forest and Santa and the Spirit of Love in the World. At the end of each song everyone clapped, and conversation buzzed around the table until the next performer stepped forward.

When the clock struck twelve, the party ended. The guests bade their host farewell and departed. The Duke suggested that Peter and Amy should try to get a good night's sleep because tomorrow they would be taking their trip to North Pole. Although the thought of visiting their old friends was quite exciting, they were so weary they quickly fell sound asleep.

It was not until a servant entered their room and drew back the heavy velvet draperies letting the morning sunshine flood in that Amy and Peter awakened. Once they recollected this was the day of their trip to North Pole, they bounced out of bed and quickly dressed. However, when they joined the Duke for break-fast, he had a very serious look on his face.

"My friends," he said, "we have just received a message from Santa. Klutter and Klatter have run away and nobody knows where they are. We fear they may be off to meet King Klutch somewhere in the Great Forest, or perhaps even in the Gnome Kingdom. There they will try to take over the government from King Kynd."

"Or they may be in the Valley of the Trolls, hiring an Army," suggested Peter.

"We have posted more guards and have warned every citizen to keep a sharp look-out and to report to me anything unusual."

After breakfast the Duke led them through many rooms and halls to the south wing of the castle. The walls of one hall were hung with life-size portraits of men and women. Ron de Lay explained that all these people were his ancestors, and many of them had been dukes and duchesses of Granite Mountain cen-turies ago.

At last they walked through the last door and found themselves outside the stone walls in a formal garden. The April air was mild and fragrant with the perfume of lilacs and pine. The sun shone warmly and the breeze was light. There were flower beds laid out in geometric patterns, all blooming in an array of colors that rivaled those of a rainbow. Far to the east rose the highest peak of the opposite mountain range — the very place that the Duke had indicated was the location of North Pole. Amy's heart began to beat faster.

"Now over here to the left is your conveyance," said their host, as he led the children along a flagstone path and around the corner of the castle.

Before them they saw a wooden framework about ten feet high with a ladder that led to a platform six feet above the ground. Two heavy ropes stretched from the top of the tower across the valley until they were lost in a low cloud, and from one of them hung a large, thickly woven basket big enough to hold two people. There were wicker seats around the inside walls of the basket, while stored beneath the seats were small wicker hampers, whose tops were closed and latched down. Two mountaineers were standing nearby.

"Now children, if you wish to, you may climb the ladder and enter the basket. Willy and Nilly will work the pulley that will carry you over the Valley of the Trolls and right up the opposite mountain to North Pole.

"Of course, you are invited to live here forever if you desire. In fact, nothing would make me happier. But if you wish to revisit your old friends, this is the safest way for you to travel. The wind is calm; there are no signs of spring showers; so you should have an easy crossing."

"We'll go," said Peter.

"But we want to thank you, Duke Ron de Lay, for rescuing us and for the wonderful party and these beautiful clothes," added Amy.

The Duke waved his hand. "It is nothing, dear ones. It has been my pleasure to entertain you. You have an open invitation to return whenever you wish to and to stay as long as you desire."

They all embraced, and then Peter and Amy mounted the wooden steps of the ladder and climbed into the basket.

"Be sure to hold tightly to the handholds — all the way across the valley," warned the Duke. "Sometimes there are sudden gusts of wind that may blow the basket and make it sway." He had an anxious look on his round, jovial face.

"We will," promised Amy, scarcely able to contain herself until they got under way.

"They are expecting you," called the Duke. "I sent them a message by carrier pigeon at dawn that you are coming today."

Then Willy and Nilly, who were very tall with broad shoulders and strong arms, untied the moorings and began to work the pulleys.

"Good-bye," called the children as the basket moved rapidly away from the mountain top and out over the treetops below.

"Take care — hold tight — and God's speed," the Duke called, his voice becoming fainter with each word as they rapidly swung away from Windchime Castle.

"This is fun," cried Amy as she ventured to look over the rim of the basket into the mist-draped valley below. But her voice was lost on the wind that swept round the mountain. Willy and Nilly, both busily working the pulley, and the Duke who kept watching and waving to them, were becoming smaller and smaller as the basket carried them away toward the middle of the valley.

"They look almost like Lilliputians now," Peter mused aloud.

"What did you say?" asked Amy.

"Nothing," he replied. For some time they bounced along enjoying the fresh spring breezes and the warm sunlight. They were more than half way across the valley when suddenly Peter cried out:

"Look! Look at those great big birds! They're as big as eagles and they're heading right toward us!"

"What shall we do?" cried Amy.

The birds had savage looking beaks and a wingspread of seven or eight feet. They quickly drew close to the basket and circled around it.

"Don't do anything," warned Peter. "Just sit very still and maybe they'll go away."

"And maybe they'll eat us up," replied Amy.

But the birds ignored the children. They were much more interested in the ropes which attached the basket to the pulley. They kept plucking at the coarse fiber with their beaks and croaking hoarsely something that sounded like this:

Kuk te kord, Krab te treds
Kawk te nests, Krawk te beds
Te chicks te rak, Kar balty heads.

As the monstrous birds continued to pluck and squawk, Peter suddenly realized their grave danger. Just then one of the eight ropes broke in half, and a minute later the beak of another bird bit through a second.

"Hey, shoo, you crazy birds!" he cried, as the basket tilted toward the valley below. He quickly removed his tunic and waved it over his head to scare away their attackers. The birds, however, bit at the ropes more savagely than before.

"Peter," cried Amy, as the basket tipped crazily to one side, "do something!"

"Remember what Ron de Lay said," cried Peter as he dodged a wing. "Hold tight to the handholds."

The birds did not go away. The basket bounced around in the air high over the treetops that pierced the mist below. Then to their horror, the biggest bird bit through the last rope and with raucous cackles they all flew away as the basket began its sudden drop.

It had not fallen ten feet before a circle in the center flew up above the children's heads and began to open. Like a parachute it inflated with air, righting the basket and checking their rapid descent. Both children were too frightened to say anything, but they hung on as the basket drifted slowly downward until it entered the heavy fog and finally settled in the boughs of a fir tree.

"Good grief!" cried Peter, when it finally came to rest at a precarious tilt on a bough of the tree, "we must be in the Valley of the Trolls!"

"At least we have made it half way to North Pole, and we didn't get eaten by the birds or smashed by the fall," consoled Amy.

"Duke Ron de Lay's version of a parachute worked well enough to save our lives. Wonder why he didn't mention the birds? Now all we have to do is climb down from this tree."

"We can't even see the ground," objected Amy as she looked over the edge of the basket at the dense green growth beneath them.

"Never mind; we'll climb down together very carefully. Well, come on, we can't stay here you know."

He put one leg over the side of the basket nearest the trunk of the tree, and holding firmly to a bough above his head, extended a hand to his younger sister.

Together, with great caution, they descended from bough to bough until they finally saw the forest floor a few feet beneath them. When their feet were once more on the ground, they hugged.

"We made it again, Peter."

"No broken bones at least; just some scrapes and scratches."

"And look at our lovely clothes," Amy cried. "My right sleeve is ripped half way out."

"Better your sleeve than your arm. These clothes weren't made for tree climbing. Our jeans and sweat shirts would have been better. The basket is still up there. I wonder what was in the little hampers and what kind of birds those were."

"Mean birds. And do you know, I could understand some words in their squawking, but they didn't make much sense."

"Yeah, so did I. But now we have to try to cross this valley and stay clear of the Trolls. At least Santa is expecting us. If we don't show up, the dwarfs might come looking for us."

"Let's get started," agreed Amy. "It must be a long walk from here to the mountains."

Chapter 15
In the Valley of the Trolls

PETER AND AMY LOOKED FOR A PATH, but they could find no trace of one. The evergreens above their heads were so tall and the branches so dense, they could not see the sky. The mist that hung over the valley obscured the sunlight; so the forest was quite dark, making it impossible to guess the position of the sun.

"Which way should we walk?" Amy asked.

"Who knows? We'll just have to take a chance. Seems to me we came down on the side of the tree nearest Granite Mountain. The basket is hanging on this side. So we'll go to the opposite side of the trunk and walk away from it."

Because there was so little sunlight, there was no under-growth of bushes or vines, so the walking was fairly easy. The lower limbs of the trees were trimmed off to a height of about five feet. Peter observed this and realized there must be trolls in that part of the forest who were keeping the woods clear enough that a short person (or whatever a troll is) could easily move through it. He did not mention his observations to Amy, however, for fear of making her more frightened than she already was. But he removed his pen knife from his pocket and proceeded to cut some tree bark from every sixth tree they passed.

"Why are you doing that?" asked Amy.

"This is a blaze," replied Peter. "I'm blazing every sixth tree to make sure we don't walk in circles or retrace our steps, like they taught us to do in Boy Scouts."

"But the trolls will see those marks and follow them to where we are."

"True, but we'll have to hope we can move faster than they can."

71

"Or that we're not walking right into a troll town, or whatever they have."

They continued as fast as they could for about an hour, when the forest floor began a gradual slope downward. They eventually came to a wide running stream. The stream bed was filled with large rocks, and there were boulders along the banks.

"Well, here's something," said Peter. "We may have reached the center of the valley. See, the ground begins to rise on the opposite side of the stream. Perhaps we are moving closer to North Pole."

"I hope you're right. At least we haven't been here before."

Peter knelt down and cupping his hands, dipped them into the flowing water.

"Ah, that tastes good! Try some."

The children drank and washed their scratched hands and faces. They were soiled from their landing and long hike but not warm, because the forest was cool and damp. The early spring water was icy cold.

"Okay," said Amy, shaking the water from her hands, "I suppose we'll have to cross the stream."

Peter looked around him.

"Maybe it would be best to follow the stream, since it might lead us out of the forest. But we don't know what we might find. So let's just cross and hope that the rising ground on the other side is the shortest route to North Pole."

After removing their shoes and stockings, the children stepped carefully from rock to rock until they finally reached the opposite bank. They dried their feet as well as they could on pieces of hemlock and donned their stockings and shoes again. Amy looked ruefully at the worn soft fabric of her slippers.

"I wish I had my old sneakers," she sighed. "I feel every stick and stone through these soles."

"I'll bet you do. These boots the Duke gave me are heavier than those shoes. I'd give them to you, but I don't think I could walk through this forest in my bare feet."

"Never mind," replied Amy. "I'll manage."

Now they were on rising ground, so they were forced to walk more slowly. Thus far they had seen and heard nothing more than bird calls above their heads, the chatter of squirrels, and an occasional glimpse of a deer or doe which disappeared into the trees at their approach. But suddenly they heard a very familiar sound. It was the mewing of a cat quite nearby.

"Listen to that!" cried Amy. She hunted in all directions behind bushes and in little ditches without success. "Where in the world is it?"

Peter was standing back looking around him.

"You can't see it, Amy, because it's over your head," he replied with a chuckle.

Amy quickly looked up and there above her head was the furry golden face of a tiny kitten. Amy laughed at the cute little face peeping through the evergreen branches.

"He must have climbed the tree and now he doesn't know how to get down. Come on! You can do it. Just let your tail come first. Swing around! There, now see! Your claws will hold to the bark. Come on, now — one more branch."

The kitten slipped and clutched for the nearest tree limb.

"Meeeow," he wailed. He was now caught in the crotch of a limb and flailing the air with his paws.

Peter stood on tiptoe and managed to reach him and pull him down. When Amy cuddled the little fellow in her arms, he began to purr and smile at Amy with an expression of love and gratitude in his opal eyes.

"Isn't he adorable?" cried Amy. "I don't think I've ever seen such a pretty kitten."

"He's cute," agreed Peter. The kitten was a pale yellow that blended into a rusty orange with orange stripes on his face and orange rings on his tail. His muzzle was white and the inside of his ears was pink. He had a deep pink nose and pads and bright pink lips.

"I wonder if he lives here?"

"Put him down and see what happens."

Amy gently placed the kitten on the ground. He scampered off among the trees, but quickly returned, looking up at the children with his bright, oval-shaped eyes.

Amy picked him up again and studied his little face.

"His whiskers are all white except one that's black," she observed. "Black and white — does that remind you of someone?"

"Homer! Do you suppose it could be Homer's lost kitten?"

"Is your name Rosebud?" asked Amy.

"Meeow," replied the kitten.

"We have to be on our way," said Peter. "See if he will follow us."

When they walked away, the kitten showed no signs of leaving them. After they had traveled another hour or so, they began to feel both hungry and weary.

"We'll have to rest a few minutes." said Peter reluctantly. The walking was difficult now, and the children were fearful because the scenery never changed, and they could not be certain that they were traveling toward North Pole or just wandering off in some other direction.

They sat down at the foot of an ancient hemlock tree. The kitten lay down beside them. They didn't talk because they lacked energy. Amy was recalling all the fairy tales she had read of children lost in forests. Suddenly she had the feeling of someone looking at her. She glanced around in time to catch a glimpse of a figure lurking behind a tree.

"Peter!" she gasped. "We are not alone. Something is behind those trees."

"Probably a deer," replied her brother.

"In a red cap?"

Peter jumped up.

"Let's move on," he whispered.

Amy picked up the kitten and held him firmly in her arms. The kitten was frightened enough to snuggle closely against her. With pounding hearts they moved rapidly through the trees. They had walked only a short time when they noticed that the forest was getting much brighter. More sunshine was streaming through the trees than before, and the trees were more widely spaced. Bushes and vines were abundant on the forest floor.

Soon they saw the reason for this change. They passed a number of stumps, some old and rotting and others that were freshly cut.

"There must be trolls around," whispered Peter.

The forest grew brighter and brighter, and ahead of them they could see open land. Suddenly from behind the thickets and trees a dozen little creatures stepped out before them. They were brown and fur covered, with large pointed ears that stood erect, somewhat like those of the gnomes. Thick brown fur grew around their faces and rose from their foreheads in a kind of pompadour. It also grew along the sides of their cheeks and down to their shoulders. They had short stubby tails; their legs were short and thick; their feet were long and broad and covered with dense dark fur. Their pale green eyes were spaced widely apart. Their noses were large and turned up, and their front teeth protruded like a beaver's. The only clothing they wore were bright red knitted hats. Each troll carried a roughly hewn club in his right hand.

"Great jumping beans!" cried Peter. "Now what?"

The trolls stood looking at the children. Finally one stepped forward.

"You come," he motioned to Peter and Amy.

A troll stepped forward. "You come!" he said to Peter and Amy.

Chapter 16
The Troll King

AMY FOUND HER VOICE: "We're Peter and Amy Landon. We were riding over your valley in a basket to visit Santa Claus in North Pole, but the ropes broke and we landed in your trees — quite by accident. We don't have time to visit with you now, but thank you for your kind invitation. Perhaps another day. We'd just like to get to North Pole as quickly as possible. Are we walking in the right direction? If not, would you be so kind as to show us the quickest route?"

The trolls looked at each other and then back at Amy. The leader stepped up close to Amy.

"*You come!*" he said.

"They probably didn't even understand you," said Peter.

But Amy stamped her foot.

"*Not come!*" she revised her speech. "We go North Pole. You let us pass! *Now!*" Her eyes flashed.

The trolls began to giggle and then to laugh. They rocked back and forth with merriment. Two of them turned somersaults. They laughed and laughed for so long that Peter and Amy began to move away toward a group of trees off the the right. Then the trolls stopped laughing and surrounded the children. Raising their clubs over their heads, they said in one voice, "*You come!*"

"We'll have to go," whispered Peter. "We can't fight twelve animals, or whatever they are, with clubs and teeth like that."

"At least they talk," said Amy.

"A little," returned her brother. Then turning to the trolls, "Okay, where do you want us to come?"

The trolls, pleased at their victory, led the children out of the forest and along a narrow, rock-strewn dirt road. Ahead they saw a village of weather-beaten wooden shacks. There was a wide clearing between the two rows of houses, and all the trolls — men, women, and children — were waiting to see the strangers. Fires were burning beside the shacks while kettles hung from tripods over the glowing coals. Strange odors came from the pots — aromas that did not make the children feel hungry. The chief troll was seated on a throne made of rocks piled together. He wore a purple hat and held a gold colored scepter. He regarded the children without a smile as all the others looked on.

"Who you?" he finally asked.

"We're Peter and Amy Landon. We have been visiting Duke Ron de Lay at Granite Mountain, and now we're on our way to see Santa Claus and the dwarfs at North Pole." Amy thought it best not to mention King Klutch or Klutter or Klatter, just in case Klutch had escaped from the tunnel and been in touch with the trolls. "We would be very happy if you would just give us some bread and direct us to North Pole."

The Chief said nothing for a long time. Finally he spoke:

"*You* cut our trees. Why you cut our trees?"

"We were lost and we nicked the bark so we could be sure we were not walking in a circle," explained Peter.

"You cut our trees. Not good. Bad to cut our trees."

"*You* cut your trees — you cut them all the way down," cried Amy in exasperation.

"Only few. Not often. We need wood. You cut bark. Tree hurt. Tree cries. Tree dies."

"No it won't," defended Peter. "The bark will grow back."

"Where North Pole?"

The children were amazed.

"Somewhere on the top of that mountain ridge behind you."

"Who Santa Claus?"

Peter and Amy were speechless. The trolls apparently dwelt in their valley and never made any effort to meet or be friendly with their neighbors, or even learn who their neighbors were. How could they explain who Santa was? Peter finally made an attempt:

78

"Santa Claus is a red elf who lives in a castle on top of that mountain in a city called North Pole. All the people up there are called dwarfs. They work all year to make toys for children and gifts for grown-ups on Christmas Eve. Santa brings gifts to all the people in the world — our world — who celebrate Christmas. He brings happiness and gifts to everyone to celebrate God's gift to us, which was the birth of Baby Jesus."

"Nobody told me," said the Chief with a frown. "Nobody bring us gifts. Nobody bring us happiness. What happiness?"

Then Peter and Amy realized that the reason the trolls seemed so bad was that they lived in their dark, mist-shrouded valley and never explored the world above them; nor did any of their neighbors bother to learn anything about them.

Just then a group of trolls arrived dragging the basket that had carried the children into the tree. Peter thought quickly.

"Here is our gift to you. There are small hampers under the seats. Open them."

The troll chief walked over to the huge basket and felt it carefully. He looked up at Peter and Amy and grinned.

"What for?" he asked.

"You can store things in it, or rig up poles and pulleys and travel in it," replied Peter. Before the chief could ask what poles and pulleys were, Amy said:

"Open the small baskets that are under the seats."

Several trolls removed the woven hampers and unlatched them. The little baskets were packed with fruit and cookies and cakes and pies and sandwiches of all kinds. There were containers of lemonade, apple juice, and elf flower tea. The children gazed hungrily at the food.

"What this for?" asked the chief.

"Eat some," suggested Peter.

The chief was wary.

"You taste!" he ordered. The children were delighted and grabbed handfuls of the goodies and a container of elf flower tea. When the chief saw them eating, he tasted a cookie.

79

"Good!" he said as he grinned from ear to ear. "Give food to trolls. Save this basket for me," he ordered.

The trolls did as they were told. Soon everyone was sitting on the ground eating heartily, as they poked one another and laughed between bites.

"This good gift," the chief said to the children, "from Santa Claus?"

Peter and Amy didn't want to confuse him by saying it was *for* Santa Claus, so they just nodded as they munched on olive and cheese sandwiches.

"What that?" The chief pointed to the kitten snuggled in Amy's lap.

The children looked surprised.

"It's a kitten — a baby cat," replied Peter. "Don't you have cats here?"

Instead of replying the chief made some strange sounds to the kitten. The kitten replied with a string of similar sounds. The two appeared to be carrying on a conversation.

"You not talk to animals?" he asked.

"We can't understand their language," replied Amy. The chief shook his head.

"You make good food and that —" he pointed to the basket, "good cover," he fingered Peter's tunic. "Can't talk to animals!" he grinned. Then all the trolls began to laugh and turn somersaults until the air rang with the raucous sound. Peter and Amy were annoyed.

"Well, what did the kitten say?" asked Amy.

"Kitten say he Rosebud, son of Homer. Two gnomes steal him and leave him in our woods because Homer was why they had to be stable grooms. They getting revenge. Gnomes lost war because Homer dug up horn."

"Great jumping beans! They must be Klutter and Klatter. Does Rosebud know their names?"

"Who Klutter and Klatter?" asked the chief.

"Never mind," interrupted Amy. "Thank you for your kindness," Amy tried again. "You may keep all the baskets and all that

80

is left in them; but we would like to leave now. If you will please let us go, we will tell Santa all about you, and he will surely bring you more — many more presents."

"But if you hurt us or keep us here, he will never know what nice, uh, people you are, and so you will never receive any presents at all," added Peter.

"What 'people' mean?" asked the chief, who appeared to have heard only that one word.

"We're people," said Amy trying to smile.

"We trolls, not people. Not want to be people. We talk to birds and animals. People can't."

"You're very smart and cute and friendly," Amy flattered, "but please let us go now, because we want to reach North Pole before dark."

"You promise more gifts?"

"Lots more. All sorts of good things," Peter quickly added.

"You go. Take baby cat. It eat birds and mice and rabbits. Moles too. Not want in forest."

The children jumped up, and Peter tucked Rosebud under his arm.

"Thank you very much. We'll see that you get the gifts," he promised. The chief waved the children off as he began to devour the food from one of the baskets. All the other trolls lined up to let them pass between their shacks, and continued to watch them until they were out of sight.

Peter and Amy did not slow their pace until they had reached the foothills of the mountains. The ground was so barren and rocky that the walking was quite difficult. After climbing another hour, they finally sat down to rest.

"Whew! That was scary!" Peter wiped his sweaty, dusty forehead with the torn sleeve of his blouse.

"It was almost as bad as being in the cave with King Klutch, but not quite," said Amy; "because we knew how wicked King Klutch is, but we didn't know anything about the trolls."

"They weren't so bad after all. Just strange. Not quite human."

"Everything here is strange — either better or worse, but certainly different," mused his sister.

"Well, let's get on. We're going to have trouble getting up this mountain if we can't find a path; and there probably isn't one since nobody ever visits the Valley of the Trolls."

So with Peter now carrying Rosebud tucked in his tunic, the children began to climb the steep slops of North Pole.

Chapter 17
The Dwarfs to the Rescue

THE CLIMBING WAS VERY DIFFICULT. They pulled themselves up the slope by clinging to roots and underbrush and occasional low hanging branches. To make matters worse, the sun was slowing dropping behind Granite Mountain far across the valley, while the valley itself was already veiled in its usual darkness.

"In about an hour it's going to be dark up here," declared Peter. "We'll have to try to find a ledge where we can spend the night."

"I'm really tired, Peter. Can't we stop now?"

Peter studied the steep slope above them.

"Let's climb around these rocks just above us. There are some fir trees so we would be safer there."

"Why?"

"Because we can tie ourselves to the trunks."

"With what?"

"With this," he replied, pulling a piece of rope from his pocket. "I took a few pieces from the big basket while the trolls were grabbing the food."

"Peter, you do think of everything!"

Peter felt quite pleased with himself and accepted his sister's praise as well deserved.

"Be very careful climbing around this rock," he warned. "One slip and we could fall all the way down the mountain."

Amy looked over her shoulder and shuddered. The slope here was almost perpendicular. They tested every step and clung to any shrub or root that was secure. At last they were high enough to see over the edge of the rocks. Fortunately the boulders formed a ledge wide enough to hold them for the night. They pulled themselves up and sat down to catch their breath. A pine sapling growing out of the rising hillside provided a secure post to tie the ropes to.

By the time the sun had dropped behind the opposite mountain range, both boy and girl were secured to the tree. Then Peter reached into his tunic and lifted out Rosebud, who had slept through the entire journey.

"I'd better tie him to the tree too," decided Peter as he made a loop at one end of a piece of rope and slipped it over the kitten's head. He tied the other end to his belt. Amy watched the procedure.

"I'm really hungry and thirsty," she sighed.

"Well," replied Peter digging into a pocket, "I managed to stash away some more sandwiches and a bottle of elf flower tea. How about a picnic?"

The children devoured the supper as they sat on the ledge under the pine tree and watched the daylight fade from the western sky. Then one by one the stars came out, bright and beautiful in the deep blue evening sky. Through the mists below them they could see the cooking fires of the trolls. Then even those lights finally burned out, leaving the valley drowned in darkness. But far away a row of lights began flickering in the sky.

"What are those lights?" asked Amy.

"You know, I'll bet they're in the Duke's round tower," mused Peter. "Look's like he's working late."

"I wonder if he saw the birds attack our basket?"

"If he watched through his glasses, he must have seen our fall — until we vanished in the mist. Anyhow, Santa will know something has happened to us when the basket didn't arrive."

They were quiet for a long time. Rosebud was curled up asleep and Amy was feeling very drowsy, when out of the silent darkness they heard the faint sound of voices high above them. The sound grew closer and closer until they could make out the words:

"Hiegh hoo, ladie oo, Peter and Amy, where are you?"

The voices echoed and re-echoed.

"It's the dwarfs, I'll bet!" cried Peter. The children turned about and searched the darkness of the upper slope. High above them were the bobbing lights of dozens of little lanterns like tiny stars on the mountain, slowly descending toward them.

"Here we are! Here we are!" they shouted together.

"Don't untie your rope," warned Peter, as Amy struggled with the knot. "It's pitch black here. They have lights. Let them come to us."

It was not long before several dwarfs reached the children.

"Greetings and welcome!" cried Clever, holding the lantern high to see the children's faces. "We are so happy to find you both safe."

Clever had volunteered to lead the rescue expedition when Santa had received the Duke's message that the children were lost somewhere in the Valley of the Trolls.

"Because the climb is long and difficult, I want you to tie these ropes around your waists. They will secure you in case you slip and fall. Our strongest dwarfs are waiting at the top of the mountain to pull you up the steep slope above us."

"Here is Homer's lost kitten," said Amy, as they untied the ropes fastening them to the pine tree and attached themselves to the sturdy lines of the dwarfs. Clever picked up Rosebud and buttoned him inside his coat. Only Rosebud's head stuck out but the kitten seemed contented enough.

"Then we have a special thing to thank you for," said Clever. "There has been an organized search on during the past few days at North Pole and throughout the Great Forest. We'll send a messenger to the Gingerbread Inn at dawn to tell Grandmother Hollyberry that Rosebud is safe and you two have found him. Won't she be surprised to learn that you are with us again!"

By now all the dwarfs who had spread out over the slopes during the search for the children were gathering together at the top of the mountain. When they heard that Peter and Amy were found, they set up a loud cheer. The children were afraid at first to trust

85

themselves to the lines, but after a little encouragement they tried and found themselves moving swiftly to the top.

The dwarfs at the top were soon grasping their hands to pull them to safety. To their surprise Rondo, Santa's red horse, was standing behind the dwarfs, all saddled and ready to carry them to Santa's castle. The huge red horse nickered and lowered his head as Peter and Amy took turns hugging him around his neck.

Then Clever, Peter, and Amy holding Rosebud climbed onto Rondo's strong, broad back, and the horse was soon galloping along the pine-needled path through a vast forest of evergreens. Through the gates of North Pole they rode. Ahead stood Santa's great marble palace gleaming in the light of the moon which was just rising. Rondo took them right up the steps and into the great hall.

The children were shown to their rooms by servants, who also brought in a light supper and a change of clothing; but Peter and Amy were too weary to eat. They flopped into the comfort of their feather beds and were asleep the moment they closed their eyes.

Chapter 18
At North Pole

THE NEXT MORNING WAS COOL AND RAINING. The clouds were so low that they were almost touching the turrets of Santa's castle. Peter and Amy drew back the velvet draperies and looked out over the town of North Pole. They had never experienced a rainy day here before, but they saw that the scenery was no less attractive. There were lights in all the little cottages, for the dwarfs were busily pursuing their various vocations. Smoke came from each chimney, because North Pole was cold on such rainy spring days when there was no sun to dry up the mists and warm the mountain top.

A servant knocked and entered their room to build a fire in the hearth. Two other servants brought new clothes to replace the soiled and torn clothing they had arrived in and a tray of delicious breakfast foods. There were elfberry pancakes and ginger muffins along with several varieties of jam whose fruit came from the Great Forest. There was also a bowl of fresh strawberries and a pitcher of rich, golden milk.

The children were ravenous and pitched right into the goodies. Rosebud lapped up his saucer of cream and soon made it known that he too would like a helping of pancakes. Then he stretched out on a corner of the table and watched with great interest while the children finished their breakfast. Shortly afterwards, someone rapped at their door. It was Clever who had come to escort them to Santa and his council of dwarfs. The children's hearts were beating fast when once again they walked into the council chamber and beheld Santa Claus with outstretched arms to greet them.

"Dear, dear Amy and Peter!" cried Santa as hugs and kisses were exchanged all around. "So you have returned to the Great Forest! That is something no mortal has ever done before. And in addition to that, you have rescued Homer's little son from the trolls, who have been said to eat cats when their food supply becomes scarce."

The children were horrified at the thought of such a thing.

"It was really just an accident that we found him," explained Peter. He happened to be where we were walking. We heard him crying and saw his little head poking through the evergreen boughs."

"My dear child, nothing in life is 'just an accident'; always remember that. You are heroes once again; but what is this that Duke Ron de Lay has written to me about King Klutch? We learned of his escape from prison some time ago. We have had search parties hunting for him. Since we were unable to locate him in the Great Forest, we believed that he must have returned to the Gnome Kingdom, where he would doubtlessly make trouble some day."

"He tunneled into our state park," said Amy. Then she and Peter took turns describing once again everything that had happened to them since the day last October when they had ridden their bicycles to the park to try to find their way to the cave that had been the entrance to the Great Forest on that eventful day when they had accidentally found their way to the Gingerbread Inn. As their story progressed, the council of dwarfs leaned forward in fascination. When they had finished, Santa spoke thoughtfully:

"So we don't know where Klutch is — perhaps in your world, perhaps in ours — perhaps in the caves of the gnomes," he mused.

"We thought he was killed in the earthquake," said Amy, "but Duke Ron de Lay sent some people down the tunnel all the way back to the cave, and he wasn't there."

"And the rock wasn't in the opening where he put it," added Peter, "so he must have escaped."

"Hummmm! So it's possible he is committing crimes in your world, or hiding out in his own kingdom, or even in the Valley of the Trolls."

"What about Klutter and Klatter?" asked Clever. "They also have been missing and may well have linked up with Klutch."

"You children must stay here with us until we can find them and make sure Klutch has not rejoined them," said Santa. "We must also send messengers to the Gnome Kingdom to warn King Kynd. If Klutch is indeed here, he will try to recover his kingdom."

"He said he was going to hire an army of trolls with the money he stole from the bank," reminded Peter.

"Yes. Well, we shall have to visit the trolls and try to find out if they are involved with him," said Santa.

"I doubt that he has reached them yet, Santa, for if he had, they surely would not have let the children go," observed Clever.

"We told them about all of you and Christmas," said Amy, "but I don't think they understood anything but 'gifts.'"

"Let us send a contingent of dwarfs bearing gifts right away. We can't let Klutch get to them first. We'll post extra guards at the gates of North Pole and close them at sundown. No stranger is to be allowed in at any time. Klutch is as crafty as he is evil, and can easily disguise himself. We can't afford to take any chances. He almost destroyed us before. He will try again."

At that moment the doordwarf announced the arrival of a messenger bearing a letter which had just arrived from Granite Mountain by carrier pigeon. Santa broke the Duke's seal and read aloud to all assembled:

"Greetings: My men have captured the gnomes, Klutter and Klatter. They were waiting for the arrival of Klutch at the entrance to our tunnel. Will keep watch and inform you if Klutch shows up. Guard Peter and Amy well. Our regards to you — R. de L."

"At least we have two of the rascals!" cried Santa. "Doal, send a message to the Duke. Ask him to return Klutter and Klatter to us via basket with two guards as promptly as possible. Send our regards and appreciation for his invaluable help. So! One of our problems is solved.

"Now, Alan, will you take a contingent of dwarfs to the Gnome Kingdom to make sure that King Kynd is informed of these events. Offer our help if he needs it. And Clever, gather fifty stouthearted volunteers and descend to the Valley of the Trolls. Take gifts, not weapons; but as a precaution, carry a basket of homing pigeons with you and release them if there is trouble. It will be the first attempt ever to make contact with the trolls. They may not want the seclusion of their valley or their way of life disturbed by outsiders, even for gifts."

"They may not want friends," put in Peter, "but they sure want the presents."

"Yes," agreed Amy, "you should have seen them devour all the food the Duke sent to you."

Santa and his councilors laughed heartily.

"From what you tell me," said Santa, "they don't seem very much of a threat to any of us. We should have visited them long ago. It is better to have them as friends than foes!

"Now, Peter and Amy, enjoy your visit with us for a few days until we can tie up some of these loose ends and ascertain what Klutch is up to and where he is. Meanwhile, dinner tonight will be served at eight o'clock in the great hall. Meet us there. Now you may run along and visit anyone you wish and see all the wonderful things that my people are making for this Christmas."

Santa's eyes twinkled at the thought of all the joy and happiness he would bring into the world during the coming Christmas season.

Peter and Amy didn't need a second invitation. They said a polite good-day and ran through the halls to the great palace doors, skipping down the palace steps to the cobble stone road that wound through the town.

They first came to the cottage of the candy makers. Peppermint canes of all sizes were hanging over ropes strung from one end of the cottage to the other, while dwarf children picked them off the line one at a time to wrap each in transparent paper. There were dwarfs stirring chocolate filled kettles while others dipped globs of creamy filling into dishes of chocolate coating.

There were chocolate figures of Santa, Christmas trees, and reindeer set out on trays to harden and then to be wrapped in bright colored foil.

One of the dwarfs offered the children a chocolate mold of Rondo, for the news had quickly spread that the two children who had saved Santa Claus were once again in the Great Forest. Next they visited the cookie bakers, who turned out the most amazing assortment of Christmas cookies from their ovens that the children had ever dreamed of. The dwarf children carefully packed the sweets in beautifully decorated boxes and tins, which were stored away until the coming Christmas. Everywhere Peter and Amy went they were treated with great hospitality.

There were also pie and cake bakers all of whom offered them samples of their wares, until they were both beginning to feel slightly ill. However, they turned into the next street where they found the toymakers living and working. Here there was enough to keep them happily entertained for hours. There were dolls of every size and description. Amy was entranced and couldn't decide which one she liked best. Peter found the mechanical and high-tech toys to his taste. But most of all he enjoyed looking at all the new sports equipment, daydreaming about having some himself and using it on the playing field at school.

They finally arrived at the very last cottage and discovered it to be the home of Blossom and Bud Flowers, the two little dwarf children who had discovered Homer and taken him home with them. Blossom and Bud were a little shy around Peter and Amy who were so much larger and were famous. But Peter and Amy were so happy to meet the little dwarfs that their obvious pleasure and friendliness soon put their hosts at ease. The children told Bud and Blossom how they had found Rosebud and how they had learned from the trolls that he was the little son of Homer who had been stolen by Klutter and Klatter, because Homer had dug up the Golden Horn and saved the Great Forest from the conquest of King Klutch and his gnomes.

"If Rosebud needs a home, we'll be glad to take him in," said Mrs. Flowers.

"Oh, Mamma! Yes, yes!" cried Bud and Blossom together.

"But I imagine he would rather be at the Inn with his mother and father," suggested Mr. Flowers, with a tiny frown from Mrs. Flowers.

Peter and Amy felt a little embarrassed. They didn't know what Rosebud wanted. But Amy said:

"We'll ask him. He may want to go home for a while, because he is so tiny. But when he is older he might be very happy to visit with you."

"We'll tell Santa," encouraged Peter. "He'll be able to work out something."

"Goody, goody!" cried Bud and Blossom, jumping up and down and clapping their hands.

The Flowers made stuffed toys, as did most of the dwarfs who lived on their road. They led Peter and Amy into their shop where there were shelves lined with every kind of stuffed toy imaginable from dinosaurs to squirrels. There was so much to see that by the time Peter and Amy left that cottage it was nearly six o'clock.

"Boy, am I tired!" said Peter as they turned down the long road back to Santa's castle.

"Me too," agreed Amy, "but hasn't this been a wonderful day?"

"Yes. I guess we earned it through, when you think of all the terrible days we've had lately. I wonder what we'll have for supper tonight."

"How can you feel hungry after all the stuff we've eaten today?"

"It's easy," Peter replied with a happy grin. "Eating makes me hungry."

While they were dining that evening in the banquet hall, word arrived from Alan that he and the other dwarfs were being entertained by King Kynd and his Parliament. They had found no threat of harm, for the gnomes were delighted to be rid of King Klutch. They were enjoying life in their caverns and their new vacation cabins above ground in the Great Forest. They had no further desire to destroy the Spirit of Christmas, especially now that Santa visited them every Christmas Eve.

"Now the only problem we have yet to solve is how to get you children home again. The Duke has — rightfully — sealed up the tunnel you came here by. It is a long time until Christmas Eve when I can enter your dimension. Meanwhile, your parents are beside themselves with grief." Santa looked thoughtfully at Peter and Amy. "How do you both feel about going home?"

"We want to go home," replied Peter slowly, "but we don't want Mom and Dad to think we're lying or we're mentally ill and making up everything we tell them."

Santa regarded the children intently.

"You will not have any trouble like that this time, little ones. That I can promise you."

"How do you know, Santa?" asked Amy.

"Dear child, I have to know a great many things. I cannot always explain *how* I know them."

"Well," asked Peter, "how *are* we going to go home?"

"There is one more way," said Santa with a merry chuckle. "Grandmother Hollyberry has a special friend who may be able to help you. Would you like to visit her?"

"Would we ever!" cried Peter.

"Yes," agreed Amy, "in fact, that is what we were trying to do when this whole adventure began."

"Then tomorrow you may go. You'll be safe now that Klutter and Klatter have been caught. You may ride Rondo who can out-run any enemy — even old King Klutch. You may also take Rosebud back to Homer and Patches, his Mother."

"Bud and Blossom Flowers want to adopt Rosebud. We promised we would ask you about it," said Peter.

"Rosebud belongs with his family at the Inn," replied Santa, "but I shall get them another kitten they'll like just as well."

So the next morning the children bade good- bye to Santa and Clever and the other dwarfs and climbed upon Rondo's back for the long journey down the eastern slope of the mountain and through the Great Forest to the Gingerbread Inn.

Rondo waded into the water and swam across with ease.

Chapter 19
Return to the Gingerbread Inn

EVEN THOUGH RONDO TROTTED AT A BRISK PACE along the switchback trails down the eastern slope of the mountain, the trip to the Gingerbread Inn was a long day's journey. By noon they had reached the wide river which they had walked across when it was frozen nearly a year and a half ago. Now it was flowing gently between its banks. Rondo waded into the water and swam across with ease.

On the opposite shore the Great Forest spread out as far as the eye could see. It was not a gloomy, mist-shrouded forest, however, like the Valley of the Trolls. Shafts of sunlight filled it with warmth and cheer. Patches of wild flowers, azaleas, and elfin delight bushes flooded the woods with the fragrance and beauty of spring. They trotted past a cluster of little cottages which the children believed must be the vacation cabins of the gnomes. Gnome children were sailing toy boats in a pond, while others were picnicking along the river bank with their parents. A few old gnomes were sitting together on the bank fishing, a new hobby for folk who had spent their entire lives underground.

By the time Rondo trotted up the lane to the Gingerbread Inn, the sun had set behind North Pole. While a rosy glow still lingered behind the mountains, the sky to the east had deepened into a deep blue light sprinkled with the earliest stars. Grandmother Hollyberry was standing in the doorway watching for them. A plume of smoke rose from the chimney carrying the fragrance of the wood fire mixed with the spicy aroma of gingerbread into the air. All the old memories came rushing back to Peter and Amy. They could scarcely wait for Rondo to stop before they slid off his back and were embracing their old friend.

"Come in, come in," she cried, unable to control her tears of joy. A wood sprite who worked for her took Rondo's reins and led him to the stable behind the Inn.

"Feed Rondo and rub him down — and give him some of those apples in the barrel," she called as she closed the door behind the children.

"Here's Rosebud," said Peter, as he pulled the kitten from his tunic and placed him upon the floor. Homer, who had returned to the Inn, jumped down from his hideout behind the mantel clock, and both he and the kitten were touching noses and rubbing against one another and then actually embracing.

Just then Patches entered the kitchen and began to lick her baby boy. The children were on the floor petting all of them, while the older cats rubbed against them and touched the children's hands with the tips of their tongues to show their affection and gratitude.

"My dear little friends!" Grandmother cried, "How good it is to see you both again! Tell me everything that has happened to you since you left North Pole in Santa's sleigh on Christmas Eve."

It was a long story, but the children once again recounted everything that had happened to them, from their desire to visit her and their accidental discovery of King Klutch to their final rescue on the mountain by Clever and the other dwarfs.

"How fascinating it all is!" she exclaimed, as she put supper on the table and poured cups of elf flower tea.

"Santa says you have a friend who can take us home," ventured Amy.

"Do you want to go home this time?"

"Yes, I guess we do," sighed Peter.

"Your parents will probably not believe any of this either. What will you do if they want to take you to the — what did you call them — the brain doctors?"

"Psychiatrist," supplied Amy.

"It would be great to stay here with you forever," said Peter, "except —"

"Except what, dear Peter?"

96

"Except — well, we're mortals, you know. We're different from everyone here. Bad things happen to us, but good things sometimes happen, too."

"Like — ?"

"Like making the baseball team, and going to school with friends, and going to college. We couldn't do all that here."

"And singing in the school musicals," added Amy.

"What about your parents' disbelief?"

"I don't know. Maybe they'll be so glad to have us back this time they'll believe us.'

"But perhaps they will think you ran away deliberately and punish you severely."

"Yeah, It's a chance they might."

"Well, remember, Peter," put in Amy, "they must have found the door battered down and Blaze locked in the pantry. If we had just run away we wouldn't have done that."

"That is certainly true," mused Grandmother, "and perhaps they have even found King Klutch, since there appears to be no trace of him here."

"Yes, and his car. They might have found that in the park."

"He could have driven away in that," objected Peter.

"But Peter, he was really hurt. I thought he was killed," cried Amy. "Maybe the police found him in the cave and took him away."

"Gnomes are almost indestructible," said Grandmother, "but dead or alive, that would be the best of all possibilities. However, we're not sure this is true. Klutch is a tough character who will be hard to destroy.

"But I do have a message here that arrived by carrier pigeon several hours ago." She took a piece of folded paper from her apron pocket and spread it out upon the table. "Santa has located your house and family on his magic screen. They are all very distraught. They believe you were both killed during the earthquake. If you return, they will very likely be so glad to see you again that they will not harm or punish you in any way.

"In any event, when we have finished dinner, we will sit by the fire and I will try to explain some things to you that will help you to understand your parents."

After dinner they gathered before the blazing logs. The boy and girl sat on small foot stools. Grandmother Hollyberry settled into her favorite rocker. Homer curled up on his pillow by the hearth. Rosebud slept soundly in Amy's lap, and Patches sat by Peter, who was scratching her ears.

"There are two kinds of reality," their hostess began. "There is the reality that you mortals live in, such as houses, cars, cats, food — in fact anything that you can touch, taste, feel, or see, or hear. You believe in a reality that your senses perceive. You can't see the wind, but you can feel it, so you believe in wind. You can't see music sung or played at a distance, but you can hear it. So to mortals these things are real, or true.

"Many centuries ago mortals believed in many things they could not see, or that they saw very infrequently. They believed in elves, fairies, trolls, gnomes, dwarfs, water nymphs, and wood sprites, and many other such creatures. But since modern people have lost their ability to see these beings and others like them — satyrs, unicorns, and dragons, they deny that they ever existed. Indeed, they have lumped all accounts of such creatures into something they call 'myths' or 'fairy tales,' until the word 'fairy' has taken on a meaning of false or untrue or simply, not reality.

"Of course children naturally believe in all these things, even as you, Amy, still believed in Santa Claus when you arrived at the Gingerbread Inn last year. But Peter, you may remember, scoffed at the idea of Santa Claus. His culture and his education had already taught him that these beings were not real."

"But Peter was wrong!" cried Amy, "and I was right!"

Peter squirmed.

"Yes, you were, dear child; but the Santa you believed in was very different from the real one. Notice I have used the word 'real,' haven't I?"

"That's because he *is* real," cried Peter.

"You see, you have learned something about that other reality that most mortals no longer understand. It exists, although it is quite different from what you read in popular tales. We don't go around changing mice into horses or pumpkins into coaches, and Santa does not bring toys to good children and switches to naughty ones."

"No, he's not like that," mused Amy.

"No," sighed Grandmother. There was a long period of silence as everyone reflected upon what had been said. Then Peter spoke.

"Maybe we shouldn't tell Mom and Dad what actually happened to us."

"Perhaps you should see what sort of mental condition they are in before you burst forth with this tale. If something has occurred to make them realize that you have been speaking the truth, then tell them the whole story, but a little bit at a time, so they can digest it gradually."

"But suppose nothing like what you say *has* happened, and they think we're lying again?" asked Peter.

"If they refuse to open their hearts and minds to you, try not to be disturbed. Above all, do not argue with them or behave in a rebellious way. It is difficult for grown-ups to change the views they have built their lives upon. They hold these views dear, even though such opinions may be wrong."

"In other words, we should just 'play it by ear'?" asked Peter.

"What do you mean, 'play it by ear'?" asked Grandmother Hollyberry in surprise.

"He means we can't decide whether to tell or not to tell until we see how they act toward us," interpreted Amy.

Grandmother Hollyberry laughed.

"Such a funny saying! But yes, Amy, that is exactly what I do mean. The main thing to remember is not to upset them or let them upset you. You can control what happens if you understand what I have tried to tell you."

The children nodded their heads thoughtfully. There was another long period of silence.

"There are many wonders in our universe, and you have been fortunate enough to see creatures and participate in adventures which very, very few mortals have ever experienced even a glimpse of. You know many things that others have no knowledge of.

"If your family and friends do not believe what you tell them, lock these secrets in your heart, for they are the losers, not you. You will have wonderful stories to tell your children and grandchildren, and you will share a special knowledge which will delight you both when you discuss these events with one another.

"When you are old, you will think about all this with great pleasure. Be assured, no one will ever be able to make you forget your visits here."

The blazing logs in the hearth had turned into gray ashes with only an orange glow signaling the fire within. The Inn was cooling off and Amy shivered.

"It is time to retire," observed Grandmother Hollyberry, as she rose to bolt the heavy oaken door. Tomorrow I shall tell you how you may go home when you decide to leave. Please remember you are welcome to stay as long as you like — even forever. It is so very wonderful to have you here again."

She kissed them both good-night, and the children climbed the old stairs to their room with a wonderful warm secure feeling in their hearts.

Chapter 20
Passing the Rock

THE FOLLOWING MORNING when Peter and Amy came down-stairs for breakfast, they found Grandmother Hollyberry seated at the breakfast table with a stranger. He was nearly six feet tall and quite slim. He had dark brown hair and bright blue eyes. His nose was slightly turned up, and his cheeks were very rosy. He wore dark blue trousers and a white shining shirt that reminded the children of the fabric made from clouds and sunlight.

He smiled pleasantly at Peter and Amy. Grandmother Holly-berry introduced him as Hal the fairy boatman. They all became acquainted with one another as they breakfasted together.

"Hal is the only elf, other than Santa Claus, who has any con-tact with your dimension," explained Grandmother. "During the warm seasons he ferries a boat between your world and ours only for very special assignments. If you truly wish to return to your own dimension, he has promised me that he will take you there."

"It is a risky journey," warned Hal. "We have to go to sea on my fairy boat. There are often fog, storms, and dangerous tides between here and there. If there is a shipwreck, I can return, but you, alas! Once the boat has passed Division Rock, you will be mortal again and subject to the perils of the sea."

"Do you wish to take such a risk?" asked their hostess anxiously.

The children hesitated. At last Amy spoke.

"It is so very beautiful here," she sighed, looking out the win-dow at Grandmother's flower garden, "and I know we could both be very happy with you forever. But it's like Peter says — we're really mortals you know. There are things we need to do, like growing up, and getting married, and having children, and — and — doing something good in our own world." Amy's eyes filled with tears that betrayed her mixed feelings about once again leaving this wonderful land and the friends who had treated them so lovingly.

"Then, if you are both certain of your decision, I'll pack a lunch for you. Rondo will carry all three of you to the shore, which is only ten miles from here. How long your sea voyage will take will depend upon the weather. Let us pray for a gentle southwest wind. Hal will return when he has taken you to your destination. He will leave you on a beach. You must walk inland two miles. There you will come to a town.

"Walk on until you come to a school, a firehouse, or a policeman. Tell them you have been kidnapped and you want to find your parents. Give your name and address, but tell them nothing more about us. They wouldn't believe you. Above all, don't approach strangers on the street. Remember, King Klutch may be free, and he has a long arm. He is very clever at using disguises. He will be determined to kill you if he is still alive, because you are the only people who can identify him."

A cloud had erased the bright April sunshine that had been streaming in through the window. Peter and Amy shivered.

"Drink some of this warm tea," said Grandmother, pouring the delicious brew into the children's cups.

"Let us hope Klutch has been caught — dead or alive," said Hal, sensing the children's fright.

"We'll go," said Peter. "We are sorry to go away, and we know we may never see you again. But it wouldn't be fair to our mother and father and grandmother to stay." His face expressed his sadness at the thought of leaving his old friends once again.

"You will return some day," the old lady replied. "You have made the right choice. Life is a long chain of links, each one beginning with a hello and ending with a good-bye. We must treasure each link; but the chain has to keep growing as long as we live. I shall deeply miss you. God speed you and protect you."

After breakfast the children walked through the gardens and orchards behind the Inn with Grandmother Hollyberry and Hal. All this had lain under deep snow on the children's first visit. When they reached the stables, there was Rondo, all saddled and ready to travel. Homer, Rosebud, and Patches had followed them to say a last farewell.

After the hugs and kisses were exchanged and a final cuddling of Rosebud, the travelers mounted Rondo once again. The big red horse trotted down the path that led to the dense forest. This time Hal held the reins while Rondo quickly slipped into an easy gallop along the soft dirt road that led to the sea. When they had reached their destination, they saw Ariel, a sailboat, tied to a floating dock in a sheltered cove.

With tears drizzling down their cheeks, they hugged Rondo one last time. Then they boarded the boat. Rondo wheeled about and galloped swiftly off on his long journey back to North Pole.

Hal had a helper, an old white haired leprechaun named Pad, who removed his cap and bowed deeply to Peter and Amy when Hal introduced them. He hoisted the anchor, untied the ropes, and expertly handled the sheets as Hal took the wheel. Peter and Amy donned life jackets and took their assigned seats, excited by the prospect of their first sea journey.

Soon the boat was out of the cove and on the open sea. In spite of a stiff breeze, the sun was warm and Ariel slipped easily through the waves, riding them as if she had a life of her own and was born to live on the ocean. Since Peter and Amy had never before been on a sailboat, they were fascinated by the silence of the trip. Except for the soft rushing sound of the waves against the hull and the creaking of the mast, there was a marvelous silence, because there was no engine to cause noise or vibration.

"This is really fun, Peter," cried Amy, trying to brush her hair out of her eyes.

"Yep. When I grow up, I'm going to buy a sailboat like this."

"Will you take me sailing?"

"Sure. Whenever you want."

Hal smiled.

"It's about time to break out the lunch," he called. As they picnicked they saw and felt a change in the ocean. Far ahead they could see rows of white foam rolling toward them. The water was roughening. Instead of riding smoothly over the waves, the boat rose and fell with a scary thud. The wind had changed direction, and the sun had disappeared behind dark scurrying clouds. Pad the leprechaun chanted:

> "East Wind has joined
> With North Wind, our foe,
> Hold tight, me hearties,
> We're in for a blow."

Hal held the wheel steady with great difficulty. As the force of the wind increased, blowing water drenched the four of them and threatened to swamp the boat.

"Bail!" shouted Hal.

Peter and Amy found the buckets and obeyed as quickly as possible. Ahead of them loomed a dark gray cloud that stretched from sky to sea.

"Fog ahead!" called Pad.

Hal frowned. He knew they were nearing Division Rock.

"North and East Winds always were friends of King Klutch," cried Hal, "I fear they shall try to harm you if they can."

"Why?" Pad yelled above the tempest, for he did not know Peter and Amy before they met."

"They are the children who saved the dwarfs and Santa and recovered the Golden Horn from the gnomes."

But no one heard his words because of the fury of the gale. Hal and Pad could no longer talk to each other, because they both had all they could do to keep Ariel upright and on course. Division Rock now loomed close onto starboard, a dark, ominous shadow in the drenching spray. North Wind strove with all his might to shove the boat into the rock, but Hal kept a tight grip on the wheel. Then suddenly they were past the point. Hal and Pad grinned at each other, pleased with their triumph, knowing they had once again navigated the dangerous rocks successfully.

The fog was lifting. With one furious final effort, North Wind scooped up a wall of water that struck Ariel aft and swept over the stern. Although Peter and Amy were holding tight, the force of the water broke their grip, and they were swept overboard.

Instantly the wind ceased, and the ocean began to calm down. The children, half drowned, floated upright in their life jackets, which Hal had specially designed for his dangerous crossings. A gentle roller picked them up and carried them right up onto the beach. Hal and Pad exchanged smiles, thinking the children were safely ashore. Hal turned Ariel in a wide circle, heading toward home and the Gingerbread Inn.

However, Peter and Amy lay in the wet sand. Fortunately, the tide was receding, or they might have been washed back into the sea. Gulls wheeled above them and more than one audacious bird landed to see if these creatures in strange purple shells were edible.

Meanwhile, far down the beach three figures were strolling by the water's edge looking for conchs, which are often washed ashore during violent storms.

"Look at those two sacks up the beach," said one. "Maybe something valuable has washed in from a boat."

"Yeah! Maybe pirate treasure," scoffed another.

"More like a couple of garbage bags," said the third.

"They're purple, not black plastic," sneered the first.

"They're not bags at all," said the third, as they drew nearer.

"They're people — children!" cried the second, and all three broke into a run.

Grandmother Hollyberry introduced him as Hal, the fairy boatman.

Chapter 21
Home Again

PETER AND AMY OPENED THEIR EYES SLOWLY. Each was in a metal bed in a hospital room. For the first few seconds they couldn't see anything but light. Then they saw shapes. Gradually faces came into focus. Mr. and Mrs. Landon were bending over their children. At the foot of the bed there were strange people in white.

"Hello, Mom." Peter's voice was so faint he could barely hear himself, but his mother wept and hugged her son.

"Speak to me, Amy!" cried her father.

"I'm okay, Daddy," Amy murmured. "But I'm so tired!"

"Thank heavens you are both all right," exclaimed their grandmother, who was standing between the beds and holding a hand of each child.

Peter and Amy exchanged glances and smiled.

"What happened?" Peter finally asked.

"That's what we want you to tell us," said a voice near the window.

Peter recognized Bob Johnson and Erasmus Jones along with the two men from the F.B.I.

"No questions now, please," said a young man in white at the foot of the beds.

"When then?"

"Perhaps tomorrow — we'll see, and only if they are willing and able to talk to you."

The four men turned to leave.

"We'll talk to you now," chirped Amy.

"Oh, darling, you must listen to Dr. Lieder. You and Peter almost drowned," said Mrs. Landon. "If those shell seekers had not come along the beach when they did you might not be alive."

"Where's King Klutch?" cried Peter, suddenly remembering past events.

"Where he's never going to do any more harm," replied Chief Johnson. "In jail on charges of kidnapping two children, causing bank failures by manipulating stocks, and grand theft."

"Thank goodness!" gasped Amy. "Then he didn't die in the earthquake after all?"

"He was pretty busted up when we pulled home out of the cave," said Erasmus Jones, "but no, he isn't dead."

"Then you found him and he didn't escape down the tunnel?" asked Peter

"See? I told you there was a tunnel behind that big boulder, but you kep' saying 'no, no, no.'"

"Well, when we went back to check, there wasn't one there," said Chief Johnson gruffly.

"That's because the Duke's men closed it up before you went back," explained Peter.

"Well, I'll be!" cried Erasmus. "How you know all this stuff?"

Peter and Amy looked at each other and smiled smugly.

"Did you find all the things Klutch stole and hid in the other cave?" asked Amy.

Chief Johnson nodded.

"He confessed and told us where everything was stashed, after we questioned him. He is still in very bad shape."

"How did you know where he was to begin with?" asked Peter.

"Some of your neighbors saw the car leave your driveway, and by the direction it took we assumed he was heading for the state park. We were able to find the fresh tire tracks on what was really a walking trail, and then we followed them to where the car was parked. But it was that beagle of yours who located the cave you were in by finding your belt in a wild blueberry bush at the entrance."

"I dropped it there so maybe you'd find it and know where we were. So Blaze was the one who found it," murmured Peter with a smile of satisfaction.

"That dog near 'bout went crazy," Erasmus took up the story, "snuffin' aroun', yippin' and yappin' till we got that cave open. An' there was that pile of rock with that hand and arm stickin' out, an' I knew right away you kids been tellin' us the truth all along," said Erasmus.

"Now that's all for today, gentlemen," said the young doctor. "Peter and Amy need to rest and recover their strength."

"They're heroes, you know, Doc," said Jones.

"All the more reason to take proper care of them. And shoo all of you out."

The two policemen, the agents, and a reporter who had quietly entered the room began to leave; but as he reached the door, Erasmus Jones turned toward the children and with a big smile, saluted them.

VERSES FOR MOLLY

1.

Shadows of the flying gulls
Slip silently across the beach;
They're glad to snatch the crumbs you toss,
But skillfully stay out of reach.

2.

Butterflies upon the air
Flit through zinnias and dare
To punctuate the colors there.

3.

Lady bugs go flying home
If you say in voice stern,
"Your house is on fire
Your children will burn!"

4.

The green and wriggly parsley worm
That does the farmers so much harm
Becomes the monarch butterfly.
Resplendent in its golden wings,
It soars amid the forest trees,
Above the roads, across the seas.

5.

We watch the stars from heaven fall,
Why we don't understand at all;
What makes them leave their given space
To tumble to some alien place?

Betty Stewart Behringer is a prize-winning poet whose work has been published in anthologies and literary journals. She is a native Baltimorean who grew up in a northwest suburb. She graduated from Towson State College and the Johns Hopkins University. She taught English for 20 years in Baltimore. *The Gingerbread Inn,* 1989, was her first published story book for children, and *Return to the Gingerbread Inn* is its eagerly-awaited sequel.

The Gingerbread Inn
was set in the
Goudy & Century type families
by the Image Foundry, Ltd.
of Baltimore, Maryland
in October, 1992

The Chestnut Hills Press
Baltimore, Maryland